WINGS OF A LARK

Goddess Durga Series book 4

Jen Pretty

I AM WHAT YOU DESIGNED ME TO
BE. I AM YOUR BLADE. YOU CANNOT
NOW COMPLAIN IF YOU ALSO FEEL
THE HURT.

—CHARLES DICKENS, GREAT
EXPECTATIONS

CHAPTER ONE

I pulled off my shoe and dumped sand back into the giant sandbox I had been travelling through for the last few weeks. Singh lay stretched out in the small patch of shade under a wispy tree. The feeling of something evil had been pulling me across the Indian desert, but now, it felt further and further away like a mirage. I was also chasing a literal mirage. I ran out of water the day before, and since then my lips had cracked, and my mouth was full of grit.

"Singh, I need water," I croaked. "I will die." We had already established that I wouldn't literally die. Durga wouldn't let me. The bitch.

Singh huffed and dragged his lazy ass up out of his shady spot. He was enjoying our desert adventure too much. He would catch gazelles and drag them back for me. A few times I cooked up some, and it was almost as good as bacon but really bloody. For a while, we travelled along a path that local villages used, but it went straight through small communities, and a white lion didn't blend in. So, we wandered the desert aimlessly.

The first village we passed through gave me clothes that were better suited for the desert. The people celebrated us and decorated Singh with some paint made from plants. It smelled terrible, but the work was intricate and beautiful. It had mostly worn off, but you could still see it in places.

I followed the lions switching tail through a grove of bushes and past more tall trees. Birds circled above. I wasn't sure if they were vultures, but they were big and soared effortlessly. They occasionally blotted out the sun.

Finally, we cleared a sandy hill and below was a small village. Women were pumping water at a cement well. They wore bright-coloured saris that made them brilliant against the desert background of muted beige. They filled silver pots and carried them on their heads back towards the village, their clothes flowing in the wind behind them.

My sari was blood red. Durga had preened when I put it on and checked my reflection in a small mirror. She thought we finally had something lovely to wear. I admit it was much cooler than the clothes I arrived in and I hadn't had a sunburn since I wore it.

Several camels congregated around the well, drinking from a long trough. They stomped at flies and watched our approach. There were always flies. The sun was setting, and the low angle of the fading daylight made the sand that floated on the soft evening breeze looked like mist. Some goats bleated and wandered about between the straw-roofed huts. Men in turbans sat around in circles laughing and speaking rapid-fire Marwari, which a girl at a small village told me was the most common language in this area. The camels moved away from the well as Singh, and I approached. Their long legs, bending and their toes dragging through the sand as they took each slow, lumbering step.

Singh sat in front of the trough and waited for me to pour more water into it, but I drank right from the spout, standing on the cement platform as I pumped the water. With my stomach distended, I filled the canteen I had been dragging empty for the last day and a half and then hopped down to rinse my hair in the trough. I wrung the water from my hair and replaced my scarf. A scream behind me had me spinning to find a woman staring at us. Singh stopped lapping at the water and blinked at the woman. She wore a turquoise sari, her black hair partially covered in a pink scarf. Others came running, joining her in staring at my lion friend.

"Come on Singh. Let's get this over with."

We walked towards a group of people, men, women and children. They bowed their heads, babbling words I couldn't possibly understand. Singh rubbed up against my hip as we walked through the now crowded village. People offered us gifts and food, so I sat down on a tree stump near a fire and ate some of their food. Singh lounged in the sand, the air was cooling as the sunset, and it felt nice to be around people, even if I didn't understand them.

A man stood up, and everyone quieted. He spoke in slow words with gestures and actions. It sounded like he was telling a story. The children all made faces, laughed, cheered and booed at what was probably appropriate moments. I wished I understood Marwari, but Durga was listening. She forced a laugh from my lips at one point even though I didn't understand what was going on. She was always just at my surface now. Her presence was as normal as my own, leaving me feeling empty on the rare occasion she disappeared.

When the man finished, the crowd clapped and cheered. Another man distributed small bottles of alcohol and presented me with two. I gave Singh a look. He hadn't turned back into a man since we landed in India. I wasn't sure he even could anymore, but it meant more alcohol for me. I had heard the desert moonshine could kill you, but I drank it anyway. Durga was happy with her life and not ready to let me die, so I was invincible. The women were decorating Singh with little swirls and motifs. He lay still in the sand as they worked. I sipped my liquor. He was more art than lion by the time they finished.

A woman stood in the center of the gathering, and a hush fell. She wore a vibrant pleated skirt and tons of beaded necklaces and bracelets that rattled and rang as she moved. An old woman began singing, and a man kept the beat with a tambourine. The woman with the beads danced to the music, her arms moving smoothly through the air around her. The strings of beads created more music, and she became the rhythm.

She looked like Durga, the way her arms waved and posed. Durga pushed at me to get up and dance, but I wasn't in the mood for dancing, and eventually, she relented, satisfied to watch the beautiful woman as she twirled, in a show of vitality and joy. The old woman's voice rang through the desert village for a long time. I wondered how she had the energy to sing so loud.

Deep wrinkles lined her face, and her eyes were a soft white colour that suggested she was blind. She held her headscarf over half her face as if she was hiding. At one point the dancing woman welcomed the children to dance with her, and they all leapt around with glee, twirling and falling. Some older girls copied the woman's movements with the competence that adolescence provided. The adults laughed and drank. I mostly drank.

Eventually, the music stopped, and people dispersed to their huts. The sounds dying until the crackle of the dying fire was the only noise.

The circular buildings with grass roofs looked like mushrooms in the darkness. I felt like Alice in Wonderland, but that could have been the alcohol.

Up at the sky, billions of stars twinkled. I had never seen so many in my life. There was nowhere on earth like this place. If it wasn't for the nagging feeling that evil lurked out there, somewhere far away and I had to stop it, I would have just stayed here.

When the last of the drunk men disappeared into huts, I scooted off my stump to lie on the hot sand beside Singh. A villager tried to encourage me into a small shack, but I had grown used to sleeping in the sand with my lion and wasn't ready to be civilized again, just yet.

When I closed my eyes, the world started spinning too fast. I clung to Singh who groaned and stretched. My cheek pressed into the rough sand, soaking up the heat the sun had left behind. Sleep finally dragged me under, but I dreamed of a little boy with sky-blue eyes and a smile that eased every ache in my heart.

When I woke, my mouth had become the Thar Desert. My teeth were gritty with sand, and my face felt like Singh's rough tongue had scrubbed it. I swung my arm around and realized my lion was missing. Oh well, one less bloodthirsty predator to worry about.

My hand fell on the plastic canteen I would recognize anywhere, it had become more than just my latest accessory; it was my lifeline in this parched land. I unscrewed the top and took a deep drink of the fresh water inside. It always tasted like plastic, no matter how fresh the water was. Chemicals were probably leaching out of the man-made container.

I forced my eyes open, though my eyelids scraped over my eyeballs like sandpaper. I could hear children laughing, and as I sat up, I found my lion. Adorned in bright colours and jumping around with the children, he was playing some game. It looked like tag. I wondered if people in India played tag or if that was just an American game. I stood up and stretched, letting half the desert fall out of my sari. The wind blowing from the west swept it away or was that the east?

Singh glanced back at me before continuing his game. Adults looked on, watching their colourfully dressed offspring pull the lion's tail with glee. They would need to explain to the children not to try that with any other lion.

I slung the canteen strap around my body like a purse. I carried nothing else with me, no ID or credit cards. I cut them up when I left the airport. Singh and I were off the grid.

"I know English," a young man said as he approached me.

"Good, have you seen Mahishasura?" I asked.

His eyes went wide, and he stopped dead.

I watched him, waiting for an answer. When he seemed to snap out of his shock, he shook his head.

I turned to go, but his next question stopped me again.

"They ask you of the king?"

A thick knot gripped my throat, but I swallowed it down and answered. "I don't know any king." I turned to begin the next leg of my voyage east. Or was that west?

"They say he came. He is in India," the young man called as I walked away. My heart begged me to turn back and ask him what he was talking about — get confirmation — but my legs kept walking me away.

A woman caught up before I left the village and handed me a bundle of cloth. I knew it was a clean sari as soon as I saw the beautiful colours and patterns. It was a bold red like the one I was wearing but had a paisley print to it, and the scarf had a gold thread running through it.

I thanked her and continued walking. The unseen chain that pulled me towards evil kept dragging my steps forward. Singh's purr startled me out of my thoughts a few minutes later. His face rubbed against my hip, and I threaded my fingers into his thick mane. I wasn't even sure why I was still going on this journey. Sure, I vowed to rid the world of evil. Not like I had anything better to do, I suppose.

The day wore on. The sun beat down until it was too hot and we had to rest in the shade for a few hours. I undid the bundle of cloth the woman had given me, unfolding the beautiful sari. In the center of the mass was flatbread I had eaten the night before around the fire and another bottle of desert moonshine. I ate the bread sitting in the shade. It was delicious. I couldn't compare it to anything else I had ever tasted, and it was, hands down, better than the gazelle that Singh caught. I stripped and changed into the clean clothes. Only Singh was around, and he was too busy chewing on bones to care about a naked woman. The clean clothes were almost as good as a shower. I missed showers. Hot water. Soap.

When the sun passed its peak, we walked again. The sand filled my shoes making my feet feel like they were on fire. I sometimes wondered how the soles didn't just melt on the boiling sand surface. I wondered many things as we walked. None of the things I thought about mattered, but they occupied my mind.

We crested a rise and before us was a ghost town. During our time in the desert, we stumbled on two others like this one.

We walked quietly, as though if we were loud, we would wake the dead. Families had once occupied the tiny village, now all that remained was sand. Scavengers had already picked the bones clean. A few still lay bleaching in the sun. The huts were burned, leaving nothing but soot in circular patterns to mark the places where people once lived.

A scavenger bird circled above, waiting for us to leave so it could return to pick at what little remained. Singh and I stopped at the well. I pumped it a few times to get enough water to continue our journey. Then we left the village behind. I knew it was Mahishasura. His rampage left a trail across the desert. It added fuel to the anger that still swelled inside me. I would kill that demon.

I didn't look back as we walked. I had somewhere I needed to go, at least that was what I assumed since Durga wouldn't let me stop.

I climbed a small rise of loose sand. My shoes slipped and skidded. From the top, laid out before me was a beautiful section of pristine dunes. The wave pattern took my breath away. It stretched as far as I could see with no break of trees or shrubs.

"Looks like we'll be walking all night, Singh."

He huffed. My sneakers and his big paws broke the sand's perfect surface as we moved on towards our destination.

Where ever the hell that was.

CHAPTER TWO

The moon rose as the sun fell, turning the desert into an unearthly world. My shadow rippled across the dunes, mesmerizing me.

"You know, we could die out here," I said, breaking the silence. It wasn't the first time I made the morbid observation.

Singh huffed. I took another sip of the alcohol the nice lady in the village had stuffed in with the food and clothes. I sang that song about the guy who rode through the desert, except I changed the word horse to lion. My laughter would have scared away birds and small animals if there had been any. Singh and I were the only ones foolish enough to wander the Thar Desert.

It wasn't really aimless, though. Durga had her radar on full and was tracking some evil. In Durga we trust. My feet never faltered, no matter how much alcohol I drank. She kept me upright and moving towards our target.

"You know, Singh, you aren't great company anymore. I should have brought Drew. He knew how to have fun." I said, sipping the alcohol. "Or Frankie. God, I miss Frankie."

We walked in silence while I thought of getting drunk with Frankie in Moscow. That was good times.

"You know who I don't miss?" My shoe was full of sand, so I stopped and plopped down to empty it. "I don't miss Vincent. Not even a bit."

Singh huffed again, then yawned and plopped his fuzzy butt down in the sand.

"No sleeping, we are walking till morning, so we don't get stuck out here in the middle of the day." I learned my lesson last time. Durga kept me alive, but by the time I staggered into a tiny village, I was fully cooked. I nearly drowned in the dirty trough the camels were drinking from. I would have happily died that day.

Shoe back on, I rose and stretched my arms over my head, still gripping the bottle of liquor. In the distance I could hear a gentle whoosh sound, I couldn't see very far by the light of the moon, but it sounded man-made. It was too rhythmical.

"Where were we? Oh, yeah. I would be fine if I never saw Vincent again. He's a jerk." The memory of the little boy flashed in my mind again, but I shoved him away. Well, tried too. It was like the witch in the tunnels under Moscow had tattooed him on my mind.

I drained the last of the alcohol and kept walking. The rest of the night sludged by as Durga forced me feet onward and Singh swaggered at my side.

As the first rays of sun peeked over the horizon, the tall wind turbines — the source of the whooshing sound — came into view. They were all around us, towering over the desert like giant propellers. We climbed a tall dune and gazed down at what could only be a full-size city. A buzzing metropolis, with electricity and cars and people. Lots of people. There were tall buildings and rows of houses huddled together in the middle of the desert.

Between me and the city was a bright red landscape. It was fields of chili peppers, but in the early morning sun, it looked like blood running down the slope towards the edge of the city. I walked along the ridge to a gap between the fields, so I didn't step all over the hot peppers. We marched down the hill towards the city.

"You are going to have to shift, Singh. These people won't want a lion in their city."

Singh stopped walking and sat down. I turned and waited for him. His yellow eyes squinted like he was thinking really hard, but nothing happened.

"Are you trying to shift?" I asked with a laugh.

He narrowed his eyes, curled his lips back and hissed at me.

"Momma always said if you made that face for too long it would freeze that way." I sat down in the sandy soil to wait for the silly lion to find his human.

Durga pushed me to reach out to Singh, so I crawled forward and rested my hand on his head. Magic pulsed and curled from my fingers to the lion and suddenly he was a man again. He was wearing jeans and a t-shirt. I was jealous. I missed yoga pants. Not that I had done yoga or meditated while we were out in the desert. But Yoga pants are the best. Singh stood up and wobbled a bit on two legs. He opened his mouth, but it was like he had too many teeth, not quite a person. I couldn't understand his garbled words when he spoke.

"You need to work on that, buddy." I rose and turned back to the city, satisfied that my lion wouldn't scare too many people as long as he didn't smile.

Small shacks populated the edge of the city, with people just beginning to rise for the day. They came out and headed for the pepper fields or into the city. The further in we got, the bigger the buildings became. They had been built close together casting shade on every street. It probably kept the city cooler. At the far end, on a mountain was a giant fort, its magnificent arches and stone exterior lording over the city like a king. The rounded turret walls looked like a crown for a giant. The buildings in the city were square. Little odd shaped boxes all lined up. Some were painted, but most, including the fort, matched the desert sand. Sandcastles made by God.

We walked the streets, into the center of the city where people were hustling around setting up shops. As they did small dirt bikes and scooters crowded and honked. Several groups of tourists passed by, their cameras clicking. It was nice to hear American voices again, but I didn't pause. Durga had her senses on some bit of evil she wanted to squash, so I let her lead my legs. We crossed a highway, with noisy trucks and cars. They honked, and people yelled. Cows were wandering along the sides of the highway, loose. Men in turbans lined up in the shade watched as we walked past, their camels stood with peaceful expressions. We continued down a narrow drive between two buildings.

The sound of children crying and men laughing filled the air. There were way too many people living close together.

There was a man in a fluorescent vest standing in front of a rope that blocked off a path up to a temple. The air left my lungs. It was a replica of Shiva's temple. Durga rose to look out through my eyes. The man standing by the rope unhooked it and let us pass with a bow of his head.

I climbed the golden stone steps. Peace floated out the open doors. My muscles relaxed as I entered the simple stone building with lattice windows and the breath I had been holding, whooshed out along with the pain I had carried across the desert. Tears pricked my eyes as I fell to my knees. Durga receded and left me alone.

I closed my eyes and shed the weight of my sorrow and doubt. My body moved of its own free will, crossing my legs and setting my hands on my knees, palms open to the painted arched ceiling of the temple.

* * *

"My dear child, why do you weep?" Shiva asked. His face was a mask of peace. His snake coiled around his neck, its eyes closed in sleep.

"She has lost her way," Durga said, appearing like magic beside him. Her posture matched his, calm and peaceful; her extra arms swayed like she was underwater.

Tears ran in streams down my cheeks.

"Her spiritual journey across the desert did not clear her mind of the baggage she carries?"

I wanted to tell them I was sitting right here, but I couldn't find my voice.

"She learned nothing but how to hide herself away," Durga said with a sigh. "I wish that witch had kept her visions to herself. Lark mourns a child she does not have."

Shiva turned back, his eyes raking over my features. His serene face slowly morphed into a pitying expression.

"Can we go kill vampires please?" I didn't sound enthusiastic, but my voice was steady at least.

"Do you believe another journey would help her?" Shiva turned back to Durga, ignoring my plea.

"No." Durga sighed. "She must face her demons now. Have you summoned the king?"

"Wait, what?"

"I have, he is travelling the country in search of you. You must stop Mahishasura though. He will destroy everything we have built."

"Yes, I know," Durga countered abruptly. "Just make sure the king arrives. I can hardly stand to go on like this."

"I warned you not to trifle with the emotions of a mortal," Shiva said his eyes narrowing.

"Since when do you know anything about mortals? She is dull and depressing, that is only a little my fault, mostly her nature," Durga countered, giving Shiva a venomous look.

"Then just kill me," I shouted, anger covering my sadness easily.

Durga tipped her head and then vanished.

"I'm sorry, child, but you must complete the work you have set out to do. Know I will think of you as you travel. Goodbye."

* * *

Just like that, I was back in the empty temple. My tears were dry, but I didn't feel better. When I rose and turned around, Singh stood at the door, his face was unreadable, but his eyes shone yellow in the low light. He studied me like I was prey and he was a hunter. I let him. Maybe he would rip off my head and end it all.

He turned and walked back through the open doorway, and I followed along behind.

Out on the street I looked around, unsure where I should go until Durga pushed me into a jog and then a run, flashing my knife into my hand. My feet slapped the stone roads and alleyways, dodging pedestrians and motorbikes. I hadn't found a vampire in so long, the blade felt awkward.

I slipped through the back streets and around sharp corners into a narrow dead-end alley where I finally found a target for my anger. I slowed to a walk as the vampire's eyes grew wide with fear. He was a mouse trapped in a corner, being stalked by a red-eyed Goddess. I was more fearsome than a cat.

I stopped and looked at the vampire. He was tall and ugly, his skin, grey. He had a dead boy at his feet who could not have been older than my boy, Elliot, had been when I saw him in the tunnel in Moscow. I narrowed my eyes. Raising my hand, I slammed my blade down into the sand by my feet. I would kill this vampire with my bare hands.

The vampire took his shot. He ran at me, aiming to blast me out of his way. Durga backed me up though, and the vampire came to a stop as if he had run into a solid wall when he hit me. He fell backwards, and I pounced on him. His nails raked down the skin of my arms, renting through flesh and muscle to run rivers of my blood. His teeth gnashed, but my hands circled his neck and squeezed. He gaped like a fish out of water, as my fingers dug into his skin, ripping and tearing. His cool blood mixed with my hot blood to make a slippery mess.

He kicked and tried to free himself, but my anger was stronger than his will to live. As my fingers reached his sharp vertebrae, they grasped the delicate bones and pulled. The body went limp and ashy coloured. Dead vampires were more disgusting than live ones.

I pushed myself up to sitting, and a slow clap rang through the silent place from behind me.

I spun, jumping to my feet at the same moment.

"You want to go next?" I asked the well-dressed vampire who stood there.

"Please, Durga. I come in peace," the man said bowing. A turban hid his dark hair but his chocolate eyes twinkled, and his sharp teeth were on full display as he smiled at me.

Singh stood behind the man in the passageway, leaning against the wall like he didn't have a care in the world. Fucking useless lion.

"You are not dealing with Durga. My name is Lark, and if you don't tell me what you want, I will assume your words are a lie," I scowled. Come in peace my ass. Vampires were nothing but trouble. I tried to call my blade for dramatic effect, but Durga stopped me.

The vampire bowed his head again. "You may call me Nara, though the vampires call me Lord Narayan. I thank you for dealing with this little problem." He glanced down at my feet and then studied the blood still dripping from my fingertips. "I welcome you to stay in my home. You and your companion." He glanced back at Singh who was picking his sharp teeth with an extra-long fingernail. Singh was super creepy in this half man, half lion form.

"Fine, whatever, lead the way." I hoped he had alcohol. There was some prohibition bull shit happening in this area, and I wanted no part of that.

I followed him back around the corner where a whole army of vampires waited in formation.

One of them stepped forward with a bucket of water. He set it at my feet, and I squatted down to rinse my hands and arms, so I didn't scare any little children.

When I finished, Nara held out a hand to encourage me to walk down an alley beside him. Once we passed the guards, they marched along behind us. It reminded me of the parade in Moscow. Lost in the memories, I missed the words he spoke but caught in at the end.

"I'm sorry, what did you say?" I asked.

"I was asking if you had news of the king."

I scoffed. "The king doesn't matter."

The lord stared at me a moment and then continued walking. Singh cleared his throat, and when I looked at him, he raised his eyebrows. Judgy bastard. I didn't want to talk about Vincent.

We passed under a huge wall of stone, through a single vehicle wide gate. Motorbikes and three-wheeled vehicles zipped through, honking as they passed. They polluted the air with exhaust fumes making me miss the desert.

"Have any of your men seen Mahishasura?" I asked as we climbed the steep road with constant traffic, moving over for vehicles. Tourists were taking pictures of us as if they thought we were important people. I better not end up on some travel blog. I supposed, with a few dozen guys in uniform walking behind us, we did appear important. I pulled off my headscarf, letting my dark hair free. It blew around my face, but it had been so long since I had been able to wash it properly, it was a bit clumpy. I probably smelled bad too.

"I have someone travelling from the south, Vadodara, who sent a message saying he had news about the demon before he left the city. He should arrive in a day or two."

"Do you have showers here?" I asked.

"Of course, I will ensure you have everything you need to be comfortable while you are visiting," he replied.

We came to a small courtyard, flooded with vehicles. Nara wove between them and led us up a set of steps into a stone building. It was dim inside, with large lattice covered windows along the steps leading to a door. He pushed the door open, and suddenly we were in a beautiful home. It was like the world outside didn't exist anymore, apart from the muffled sound of horns honking.

"Just this way," he said, taking us through a beautiful sitting room, decorated in earth tones that matched the exposed sandstone walls — some covered in bright tapestries. They left the doors and windows open, allowing air to sweep through.

We walked down a hall, and Nara swung open a door, stepping inside. The room had a large, high bed with sheer material hanging from the ceiling. Nara flung open a balcony door, and I followed him out. Before me, laid out like a rich quilt, was the entire city. I was looking down on it from above, watching the flow of people and traffic as they hurried along between buildings.

"Jaisalmer is the only living fort in the world," Nara said, looking out across it. Music rose from down below, bells and a man's voice ringing through the streets. The people in this city wore more western type clothes. Some wore the same clothes as those in the desert, but here many men wore jeans and button up shirts.

"How long have you lived here?" I asked. He had a European accent.

"Only three hundred years. Is it that obvious?" he asked, leaning against the railing.

"You don't sound native to India," I said. His dark hair and olive skin could easily make him native until he opened his mouth.

He smiled at me. "One of my coven members sent word you were travelling this way, but he failed to mention how beautiful you are."

I scoffed and pushed my hair back from my face.

"I will have food and drink brought up; there is a shower with hot water through the other door here." He walked back into the bedroom and slid open a door, displaying a modern looking washroom. "I don't believe you were this thin before you wandered into the desert. I am sure it isn't healthy."

I looked down at myself. The sari covered me from head to toe, but I knew underneath it I was rail thin, my stomach was concave and my chest had shrivelled. My arms and legs were still strong thanks to Durga, but they were barely more than skin covering bone.

The vampire lord bowed and exited the room, closing the doors behind him. I glanced at the bed and found a lion flaked out on top, softly snoring away.

Typical.

CHAPTER THREE

The shower was gloriously hot, and someone stocked the cabinet with beautiful smelling shampoos and soaps. I couldn't read the labels, but the first bottle was probably conditioner since it didn't lather at all. I used each bottle scrubbing and then rinsing my hair under the hot spray. Eventually, I stepped out. The girl in the mirror was terrifyingly thin. I quickly wrapped myself in a big fluffy robe I found hanging on the back of the door. There was a brush in a drawer, so I set to work de-tangling my poor neglected hair.

A few curses and twenty minutes later, I had my hair beat into submission. It shone in the bathroom lights, longer than the last time I had stood clean in front of a mirror. I stepped back into the bedroom and found a tray of food on a small couch that looked an awful lot like the one Vincent had in his office back home. I tried not to think about that as I sat down and uncovered a plate of food. There were fruits and cheeses along with some bread and a bowl of grains.

I tore the bread and scooped the grains into my mouth from the bowl. I had eaten the day before, but Nara was right, I was painfully thin. I finished all the food and downed a few glasses of water before climbing through the gauzy sheer material and onto the bed. Singh was lying on his side. His soft breaths lulled me as I luxuriated on the thick mattress and cozy blankets. When I closed my eyes, I could almost imagine I was home. So, I kept my eyes closed until I drifted off to dream about my little boy.

A mighty roar woke me. I jumped up from the bed, immediately getting caught up in the gossamer hanging from the ceiling and falling on the floor.

"Shit. What the hell?" I pushed my hair out of my face and realized that Singh had someone pinned in the corner of the room. A man, his hand covering his head. He cowered like he could avoid being eaten by the white lion if he made himself small enough.

"Who are you?" I asked, angry at being woken from my dream. The man peered at me out of human eyes. He was not a vampire, at least.

"Please, I only wanted a lock of your hair. I promise I meant you no harm." The man was begging and crying. I hoped he didn't wet himself. That would be gross.

"Why would you want a lock of my hair?" I asked. When he didn't answer right away, Singh nudged him with his nose.

"For good luck," He cried

"Oh, sweety. I am not a good luck charm. Everyone I meet dies, grows to hate me or runs as fast as they can," I laughed and climbed back into the bed. "Don't eat him, Singh. It would make a mess in Nara's house." I rolled over, turning my back to the whole situation and curled in on myself, trying to force myself back to the dream of Elliot. I heard Singh huff and then the door open and close quickly before the bed sunk, and Singh's warm fur caressed my cheek a moment before his hot prickly tongue laved my forehead in a skin-searing lick.

"Singh! Bad lion! I told you not to lick me. Its gross and it hurts." I cupped my hands over my forehead, sure I would find the skin missing. Thankfully, I was still intact, but that didn't change the fact I was well and truly awake.

I heard a snicker and looked back to the door to find Nara standing there, biting his lip.

"I'm sorry. I came to apologize for the staff." The smile fell from his face. "I have fired that man. I did not expect anyone would be so bold. I promise you are safe here, Lark."

"Yeah. I have a lion, and an ancient Hindu Goddess, I'm safe everywhere. Even in the middle of the Thar Desert when it's hot enough to boil blood."

"You say that like it's a bad thing," he replied. I suppose vampires knew what I was talking about.

"Have you ever wanted to die, Nara?" I asked.

A look of shock made his features appear more exaggerated. His glowing eyes became round saucers. Singh rolled over on his back, nearly crushing me, so I had to scoot closer to the edge of the bed.

"I suppose I have. When my first wife grew old and died, I would have gladly gone with her."

I poked at Durga; she didn't rouse herself though. She was still napping in anticipation of meeting up with her arch nemesis.

"Would you like to have breakfast with me?" Nara asked. His white loose-fitting pants and a long white shirt made him look dapper, like an American man in an expensive suit. I was still in a bathrobe.

"I need to find clothes."

"I will have some brought up for you in a selection of styles." He turned and walked out the door, closing it behind him before I could say anything. Not that I would have turned him down. I was broke and would rather live the rest of my life in a bathrobe than put the smelly desert clothes back on. I should burn them after what I put them through.

I slid back against Singh and dozed for a few minutes until there was a soft knock at the door and a small older woman walked in pulling a wheeled clothing rack behind her. Clothes of every colour packed the hanging rod.

"Oh my god," I said. I was expecting a bundle of clothes like the woman in the village had brought me.

The woman had a huge smile on her face. She said something in a language I recognized as Marwari, but I didn't understand what she said. Durga took over and spoke back to the woman who then went about selecting clothes for me to try on. She pulled out loose cotton pants and tops that were all in shades of red. I guess Durga was choosing our wardrobe now.

The woman bowed and backed out of the room with a bigger smile than when she walked in. Singh hopped off the bed and followed her out. Durga slipped back into that happy corner inside me she likes to hang out in, and I rummaged through the clothes.

I found a pair of red loose-fitting pants and a long flowy shirt in stark white that looked amazing against my skin tone. I hadn't worn much white before, but I decided I should start.

I grabbed a scarf and pinned it in my hair to cover my head and wisp about as I walked. Then I headed out to find Nara.

I followed the smell of fresh bread down stone hallways barefoot. I couldn't stand to pull my old running shoes back on.

I rounded a corner and found myself in a large dining room with a long solid wood table, surrounded by vampires and one lion. Nara put a hand to his heart and said a few words in Marwari. I assumed from his gesture and the chuckles of the other men that it was a compliment.

"I said you were the most beautiful rose in the desert."

I bit my lip and slid into a seat beside my giant lion who was half on the table licking his plate clean.

A woman hustled in and set a plate and mug down in front of me. The cup was steaming and smelled like coffee. Thank god.

"Thank you," I said, surveying the food. There were tiny little triangles that looked like egg rolls. I picked one up and bit into it. Inside was potato and lentils and some spices that made it savoury. I shoved the rest in my mouth as the sounds of people speaking in the local tongue filled the silence. My eyes rolled back in my head at the feeling of my stomach filling twice in two days. When my plate was clean, the woman brought more, and I ate those too but felt like I might explode by the time my second plate was empty.

I leaned back in my chair, thankful the pants had an elastic waist and sipped my coffee. I inspected each of the vampires in the room for the first time. They all had dark hair and olive skin and spoke fluently in Marwari. A woman on the far side of the room caught my eye. Her hair was stark white, and she winked at me.

When my gaze finally made it around the table to Nara, he was already studying me. He smiled, and I got stuck in his brown eyes for a moment before turning away. The conversation continued among the men and women around the table for a few more minutes before Nara said a single word and everyone rose, taking their dishes with them and cleared out like their pants were on fire.

"What did you say?" I asked.

"I told them to get out," he said with a laugh.

"Rude."

Singh hopped down from his seat and wandered off too. He would probably find a bed to cat nap in.

"They have work to do. Your arrival and immediate discovery of a rogue vampire amongst us was an embarrassment. I would never want Durga to think we don't keep our city clean. I know what happens to people who don't mind their manners in her presence."

Durga preened, rolling under my skin like he had given her a huge compliment.

"You shouldn't say that kind of thing. She'll get a big head."

One side of his mouth crept up into a crooked smile, reminding me of Frankie, though he looked nothing like him. I was just homesick, and I knew it. It didn't have to make sense.

"I have tried to compliment you. It doesn't seem to work."

"Does that line work on women here?"

"I'm sorry," he said with a laugh. "I'm just quite taken with you."

I shook my head and drained the last of my coffee. I would probably kill for a pot of it right now.

"Can I show you my city?" he asked with a hopeful look on his face.

"All right," I said, against my better judgment. Vampires and I had a terrible history. I should probably discourage him with some horrible attitude right now. It would save us both time and trouble if I were a horrid bitch upfront. Instead, I let him take my hand and link it through his arm like the typical old-timey vampire he was. I grabbed my shoes and pulled them on, wincing at the sandy texture inside. He led me out of his home and around the building to the wall of the fort.

"This walkway goes around the whole fort," he said as we walked close to each other along the narrow path.

"The first wall kept most invaders away as the army would fire rocks at them from this walkway. But if the enemy made it up here, people would drop rocks, hot oil or boiling water from the windows and balconies above."

I looked up, and the wall climbed another three stories, making it a true fortress. No way would someone make it past both walls.

"This is the only fort that has stood against every attacker, in all of history and the only one left today that thrives."

"That's amazing."

We walked along further, and I looked over the side of the wall, down towards the city. It was nearly the same view as the bedroom balcony. I looked up, but the balconies along this section all looked the same.

Nara pointed to one. "Your lion sleeps there. Can you hear him?"

I listened and heard the Singh's snores floating down on the light breeze. I laughed and shook my head — lazy lion.

"So, what made you come here?" I asked.

"I wanted a change. The desert is beautiful, and the people here are so bright and friendly."

I nodded. "That's true. The desert villages were generous and welcoming."

"Well, that was because you travel with a white lion. They love and worship Durga. I imagine if they had been wealthier, they would have adorned you with gold and jewels."

"I would not have accepted that," I replied. We came around a curve and found ourselves in the middle of a group of tourists. Their cameras clicked. Some of them were taking videos and narrating. They said hello in Marwari, which was one of the few words I recognized, so I played along and returned their greeting.

Once we were past, Nara spoke again.

"I knew you would not accept gifts, that is why I did not give them to you, but please let me give you this?" He took my right hand and slipped a ring on it.

I looked down at the biggest ruby I had ever seen. The surface sparkled in the sunlight. The band was gold and fit my finger as if someone made it for me.

"I really can't..."

"Please? I won't try to give you anything else, just wear my ring as a sign of my devotion to you and your mission."

Durga rose, casting everything into a red light. Nara took a step back and bowed his head. "Goddess," he whispered.

"Thank you for this gift. Lark is young and doesn't understand the old ways, but I accept your token and your devotion." She raised my hand and placed it on the vampirc's head. "Be at peace, vampire, and maintain the balance, always."

She receded to her place inside me. "I'm sorry," I said.

Nara looked up at me with tears in his eyes. "Today I am truly blessed," he said. He wrapped his arms around me and spun me in a circle, laughing. "Thank you!" his lips met mine in a kiss and I relaxed into his arms. All that time in the desert made me crazy. I should have pushed him away, but instead, I wrapped a hand around the back of his head and let him kiss me on that ancient wall in the beautiful city.

When he broke away, he was still smiling and giddy. "Come, I have so much to show you."

He took my hand and walked us back to the gates of the fort, then through to the market. "You must try this," he said holding up what looked like a small potato.

"What is it?" I asked. His enthusiasm was contagious.

"It's a Langsat fruit." He peeled it like an orange; only it looked tougher. Inside was a white almost translucent looking fruit. He broke off a piece and handed it to me.

I popped it into my mouth. Whatever I had been expecting, it wasn't what I got. It was the consistency of jello and super sweet. There was a slight citrus taste to it, but it was mostly just sweet.

The surprise must have shown on my face because Nara smiled and pulled off another piece. He held it to my lips, and I opened my mouth and let him feed it to me. I wanted to give my head a shake. This was dangerous ground I was treading with this vampire. I needed to take a firm step back, but instead, I let him loop my arm through his and stroll me down the narrow path between the shops.

I had become a masochist. That was the only explanation.

"I wanted to show you where we keep the rogue vampires," he said.

"You keep them?" I asked, confused.

"Yes, they must pay for their sins." He said before turning down an even narrower street and knocking on a door.

The door swung open, and he held my hand, towing me downstairs and underground. A light flicked on, and mournful moans echoed through the long hall before me.

On either side of the hall were doors, dozens of them on each side. The rooms beyond the doors couldn't have been any wider than a single door, based on how tightly packed they were.

Nara led me forward and swung open a door on the right. My heart raced as he flicked on a flashlight and what lay before me was worse than my worst nightmare.

CHAPTER FOUR

It looked like a skeleton. Much worse than Trevor had been when I saved him. This vampire could barely move. His fingers twitched, and his bared teeth clicked, but he had decimated otherwise.

"Oh, shit." I stumbled back. "Why have you done this?" I asked, horrified.

"I am punishing them. They are rogue and murderers," he insisted, his smile changing to confusion. He swung the door wider, and Durga rose inside me to look at the sad vampire laying on the floor.

"Today the suffering ends. This is not the way, Narayan. You do not keep the balance through torture."

Nara's gaze returned to the prisoner for a moment and then swung back to me. "I did not know. Forgive me, Goddess!" He fell to his knees.

"I have not made my will clear to you, but today, you end the suffering. Gather your men and kill all who dwell here." Durga slid back into her place, but Nara remained on his knees.

"Please forgive me. I did not know."

All I could see was Trevor. I missed his smiling face and silly giggles as we watched movies with Drew on the couch. "Can we go?"

"I am so sorry. Of course, Goddess. Thank you for your grace Durga, I promise I will never keep another soul here."

"Sure," I said, hurrying him up the stairs and back to the street. "Do you have a phone?" I asked. "I need to make an international call." If I didn't hear Trevor's voice at that moment, I was sure I would have to go back own there and make sure he wasn't there. It was irrational, but I was irrational these days.

"Yes." Nara pulled a cell phone out of his pocket. "It doesn't always have reception. There is a better phone in the house."

I turned on the phone, and it had one bar, good enough. I dialled by heart and heard a scratchy ring, then a second ring. A soft voice came over the line.

"Hello?"

"Trevor?" I yelled, trying to make myself heard over the static.

"Lark?" he yelled back. "I can't believe it's you! Where are you?" he asked, his words slightly broken up, but I could hear most.

"Jaisalmer, the middle of the Indian desert," I said.

His laugh was a tinkle that made muscles relax I didn't even know had been tense. "It's so good to hear your voice," he said, but whatever he said next was too static to hear.

"I'll call you back," I yelled into the phone three times in case he could still hear me.

"Thank you," I said, handing the phone back to Nara. He still looked depressed, like a kicked puppy. I took his hand, to get that look off his face and led him back through the city towards his home in the fort.

"Is Trevor the one you love?" Nara asked as we walked up the stairs to his house.

"No, he is just my friend. My very good friend who I miss a lot."

"Is he a vampire?"

"Yes, but he is new. He had been starving himself when I found him and brought him home with me. Seeing your prisoners just brought back a lot of memories."

As we climbed the stairs to Naras home, he nodded. "I am truly sorry for my misjudgment and the pain I caused you. My men are already clearing the prison and should be done by sundown."

I nodded and left him standing in the large, well-appointed living room of his house. I found Singh laying stretched out on his back on the bed, and I curled around him. He purred as soon as I pet his whiskered chin. He rubbed his face on me, and I wished for a moment I could be the silly cat. His life was so much easier. If he didn't like something, he bit its head off.

"Can I join your lion club?" I asked.

His tongue flipped out and caught my hand, pulling it back into his mouth where he held it between his teeth for a moment. When he opened his big jaws, letting me take it back, it was all drooled on. Gross.

I wiped my hand on the pillow on his side of the bed before tucking it back into my chest. The midday sun cast a pattern on the floor through the lattice covering the window. I felt groggy but remembered that someone was on their way with news of Mahishasura. I would leave here again soon. Probably not soon enough.

I must have fallen asleep because the next time I opened my eyes, voices were yelling.

I rolled off the bed, and Durga flashed my knife into my hand. That was my first sign that shit was going down.

I set the knife down and pulled on my shoes because no matter what, I wasn't fighting barefoot. I grabbed up my knife and ran out the bedroom door to see what was happening.

Vampires filled the house — dozens of men and women with pointed teeth.

"What the hell?" I asked. Before anyone could answer, Durga pressed me to get moving. Evil was all over the city.

"Something happened in the dungeon. Our men are dead, and there are dozens of prisoners running free," a woman's voice rang out from the other side of the room.

"Move," I said pushing through the crowd until I found the source of the voice. It was the woman with the white hair that had winked at me in the kitchen that morning. "Can you fight?" The woman was not much taller than me and wore jeans and a tank top instead of the usual women's clothing but had a long knife in a sheath at her hip. She also had a glint in her eye that made me wonder if she was crazy. Her muscles twitched like she wanted to go.

"Of course," she said, unsheathing her knife and swinging it in a circle that had the men around her backing up — my kind of crazy.

"What is your name?" I asked. Durga pushed at me harder, but I wanted a team. A team of two would be fine.

"Pari," she said.

I smiled and swung my blade too. "Let's do this then, Pari."

Her teeth flashed, and we ran out of the house. Durga pushed me to go faster, so I did. The woman behind me kept up, and a moment later we came to the first skeletal rabid vampire. He had already drained at least two people in the small tea shop. Others were huddled in the back corner as the vampire tore flesh from the human in his arms and ate it. Gross.

He hissed at us but didn't drop his meal. I put a slight bend in my knees, ready to take him head-on. A blade flew past, sliding deep into his throat and he collapsed to the ground. I glanced over my shoulder, and Pari shrugged. I waited for a moment as she grabbed her blade and then we both ran, following the screams to a pair of rabid vampires who had cornered school children. The kids were crying and screaming as the monsters staggered closer.

"Hey!" I yelled. Both turned and hissed at me. Their eyes were blood red and teeth in a snarl.

I heard a chuckle behind me from Pari. I decided I liked her level of crazy in that moment as we faced down the nasty skeletal vampires. They launched themselves at us, and we went to work. My knife missed the first one's spine by a quarter of an inch. Instead, it took out his windpipe, so he gasped and bled all over the place but didn't slow. His teeth snapped next to my shoulder as I pushed him back to get a clean shot. Fallen vampires were strong even if they didn't look it and I imagined this one was old and powerful before they locked him away.

In the scuffle, I tripped on the uneven footing, and his weight came down on top of me. He wasn't that heavy in his current state, but it gave him the upper hand for a second and his teeth scraped my cheek, tearing the flesh. As he reared back to aim for my throat, I got my knife between us. As he came down, he impaled himself perfectly on my blade and collapsed. I kicked him off in time to see Pari nearly behead the vampire she was fighting with a strong slice that severed his spine.

She looked at me with blazing red eyes of her own. She was a scrapper, like me, and had taken a few bites to her arm.

"You aren't so pretty now, are you?" she said with a laugh as her eyes bled back to normal.

I laughed and packed the flap of torn skin on my face back together so it could heal.

She reached out a hand, and I accepted it, letting her pull me to my feet. We took off again, the single vampires were easy to take down, but once we killed six or seven, a group of them sprung on us together.

They shouldn't have been able to organize enough to attack like that, but here we were in the middle of a horde of feral vampires and fighting back to back. Our blades swung, killing with enthusiasm. More of the starved vampires came until they filled the small courtyard.

"Shit," I said.

"Don't worry, Durga. We can take 'em."

This vampire had a death wish. I liked it.

My blade cut through flesh and bone. Battle screams echoed from the city. I assumed other coven vampires were fighting the deranged ones too. It wasn't just us out here, but I focussed my mind entirely on the fight. I kicked one vampire away as another arrived.

I saw a flash of white. Singh had joined the fun. I caught sight of him now and then with his teeth wrapped around some vampire's neck as he shook them violently. The group was dwindling as we took care of business.

Bodies were piling up. That's when I saw a man with blond hair that I would recognize anywhere. He had his back turned, but he was swinging a sword with practiced ease. I froze, and the vampire I was fighting got his teeth around my collarbone, clamping down and shaking me like a dog. I screamed as my flesh shredded and the bone snapped.

Flipping my knife, I stabbed it towards myself, impaling the vampire and my shoulder with the tip of the blade.

A fire burned in my skin where my blade had cut me as the vampire fell away. My vision faltered for a moment. Another rabid vampire took that opportunity to attack me, but I got my knife up in time to sever his spine through his throat. He fell, and my vision shifted black again. It cleared, and I saw Vincent. His chest was heaving, but he had a look of concern in his eyes. His sword fell to the ground with a clatter, but I saw it like I was looking out at the world through the lattice on the windows of the houses here.

I licked my lips, trying to form words, but nothing was working. My legs were like Jell-o, and I swayed in the breeze.

"Durga!" Peri called, but I couldn't look away from Vincent. His blond hair and glowing eyes. It was a mirage. It had to be.

My eyes closed, and I felt my legs go out from under me.

Then there was just darkness.

CHAPTER FIVE

"Why isn't she healing?"

"I don't know!"

The voices seemed far away as if I was underwater. I tried to open my eyes, but they were too heavy.

"All her wounds have healed, except this one."

I recognized the voice, but I my mind was so muddled I couldn't remember who it was. Then the voices faded away again.

"Please, Goddess," a voice whispered. It was thick and full of desperation. "I'm sorry, Lark. I should never have left you."

Who was that? Why was I in the dark? I tried to move but couldn't. Was I paralyzed? I panicked and tried desperately to do anything. Was I dead?

The sound of a cat purring rumbled beside me. It soothed the fear, and my mind slowed, drifting me back into the dark peace.

"Lark. Wake up!" the voice was angry now.

"You may be the lord in your country, but I am Lord here. I say you let her rest and recover."

"She's not recovering, though is she?" the angry voice said. "I am taking her back to the elves. They made the blade; maybe they know why she's not healing."

A lion roared, and then someone lifted me. My muscles were loose, and my head lolled back for a moment before arms cradled me properly. "I will bring her. She is in there. She can't find her way out." This was a new voice. One I recognized. It was Singh. My mind settled knowing he had me. He would protect me — my will and determination. I let my mind drift back to the quiet place.

When I became aware again, the sound of an engine roaring filled my ears. I was being jostled and shaken.

"It's ok Lark. We are almost there," Singh said.

"Is she awake?"

I knew that haughty voice. I thought I had imagined him in the square — a mirage.

"She is aware, but she hasn't opened her eyes," Singh replied.

"I'm sorry Lark. Please forgive me," Vincent said. "I'll get you to the elves; they will fix this."

"Watch the road," Singh said.

A horn honked, and Vincent cursed. I wasn't sure why he was here, but hearing his voice made me want to open my eyes and see him. I imagined him in my mind. Saw his features and they morphed into a child's face. Elliot. The beautiful gap-toothed smile. Tiny fingers wrapped around mine as we walked down the street. Sadness came next.

"Don't cry lark. Everything will get better." Singh hadn't spoken this much since we landed in India. His teeth must have gone back to normal. He was speaking clearly.

I drifted back to sleep, safe with these people. My last thought was of Durga. I couldn't feel her at all.

"There is nothing wrong with the knife." A squeaky voice said.

"Then why did it cut her and now the cut isn't healing? Something is wrong." That was Vincent. It was his barely controlled rage voice.

"Perhaps she does not wish to continue. The blade abides her will. If she wanted to die, it would allow it."

"She has been bleeding for three days and hasn't died."

"I imagine the Goddess is keeping her alive. They do not seem joined though," the squeaky voice said.

"What are you talking about?"

"She no longer has the aura of the great Goddess. We can see the magic. It is fading from the girl. If she wishes to die that is her right. It is not for us to stop her."

Something slammed.

"You must leave here! We will not abide your temper in our home. Be gone, night creature!"

Someone carried me again.

"You should take her to the temple. Maybe the Goddess will help," I didn't recognize that voice.

"If she does not wish to go on, perhaps we should allow her the peace she desires," Singh's voice was quiet, reverent.

"No," Vincent snapped. "You will not die, Lark! You can't die! You hear me?"

I heard a car door slam.

"He will not rest until you return, Lark," Singh whispered. "I will be by your side until the end if that is what you choose, but think carefully on this decision."

Someone jostled me, and the car door slammed near me, followed by another. Who else was with us? The engine rumbling and tires over gravel were the only sounds for a long time.

As the engine roared, I considered the words I heard. Did I want to die? I wanted to die in the desert. Vultures circled above me day and night, but they would not land, no matter how long I lay in the sand and begged them to take me. I thought of Elliot. Would he be there when I died? He was in my dreams. The witch showed my future but was my future death, and I would be with Elliot then? Or was she showing me a life I could have in this world? I didn't know.

Eventually, the car stopped, and the engine died. The sound of car doors opening and closing proceeded Vincent's voice right beside me.

"Please, Singh. I have to know for sure. If she truly doesn't want this life..." his voice faltered. He cleared his throat. "Then I will accept that, but I must know."

"Very well," Singh replied. I was jostled again and carried up steps. Singh's boots thumped into a chamber where the sounds echoed. Peace flowed from all around to welcome me. It was the same as when I entered the temple in Jaisalmer.

Someone lay me on a hard surface, and a cool hand took mine, raising it to a set of lips. "Please," he whispered. Vincent.

I cleared my mind and let it travel to Shiva. It was so easy I wondered if I was in meditation or had slipped into death.

* * *

"Child, what have you done?" Shiva asked. He was peering down at me from above, his snake peeking over his shoulder.

I sat up and glanced around. I was in Shiva's temple. Open arched windows surrounded us, sand drifted against the walls and came in through the windows on the breeze.

"I don't know what I've done," I admitted. "I was fighting vampires, and then I cut myself, and now I can't seem to go back."

"Do you want to go back?" he asked.

I raised my shoulders in a shrug and looked away. I crossed my legs and sat before the God picking at my nails.

Shiva sighed. "You must decide. Death is a part of life, you should not fear it, but you have barely lived."

"I've done a lot of living this year," I said.

"Have you? You still hide away who you are. I realize Durga has been no help with her blood lust and one-track mind, but you have not even begun to live." He paused, but I didn't look up. "What of your child?" He asked.

My eyes shot up to his. "He is in my dreams. I see him when I sleep. Why wouldn't I want to sleep forever?"

"Because he does not grow in your dreams. He doesn't change. He is still the dirty boy you saw in the tunnel. Think, Lark."

So, I did. I let my mind look at Elliot in my dreams. Every time his fingers wrapped around mine, or I held him in my arms, he wore ragged clothes and had dirt on his hands and face; always the same. He would smile, and I would ignore the bits I didn't want to see. Tears fell from my eyes when I saw him now. He was my boy, but he was not. He was just an image of a boy.

"In the world of the living, that is where you belong, foolish girl." Shiva chided. "Now off you go, I have important work to do, and so do you."

I nodded an opened my eyes.

* * *

Beside me was a man on his knees, his head bowed to the floor. Behind him stood the most magnificent white lion. His eyes were glowing yellow. His lips curled.

I reached out my hand and touched the soft blond hair of the man bowing in prayer.

He jerked up, and Vincent's beautiful face was before me.

"Thank you, Goddess," he said as he lurched forward. His torso covered me, and his arms slid behind my back to drag me off the stone where I lay, wrapping me tightly in his arms. Tears dropped from his face to land on mine, mixing with my tears. I didn't know if I was crying tears of joy or sadness, but I was alive.

Lips met mine in a searing kiss. Vincent's warm scent filled my nose, and I relaxed into his arms. He rose, still holding me tightly and walked out of the temple into the bright midday sun. He swung open the door of a beat-up old jeep and set me in the passenger seat.

"I'm glad you have returned," a voice said from the back seat. I swung around, and it was that liar Alex. I called my blade to my hand and had him pinned to the seat, knife at his throat in a moment. I may have been almost dead a second ago, but I was not dead now, and this bastard locked me in a cage in the freaking tunnels in Moscow.

"Please!" he begged, his hands up in surrender. Eyes wide in terror.

"Why should I spare you? You helped a murderer capture me!"

"No, I helped you. It was important for things to play out that way."

"No, you are a double-crossing snitch!" blood trickled from a slice in his neck.

"Please, Goddess, I beg for mercy."

The blade disappeared out of my hand, but that wouldn't stop me, my hand wrapped around Alex's neck and my nails dug in.

"He did save you." Vincent's voice was bland.

"What?" I asked, not taking my eyes of the vampire who was gasping in front of me.

"Well, he suggested we bring you here, so technically he saved your life."

"Seems like a stretch," I replied.

"Perhaps. I will leave it up to you," Vincent said. His voice was almost joyful.

I released the stupid vampire and turned around in my seat. "What is wrong with you?" I asked Vincent, taking in the smile on his face. His dimples were on full display.

He shrugged. "I'm just glad to have you back." He leaned over and tried to kiss me again, but I stopped him with a hand on his chest. This bastard high tailed it, leaving me a letter. Then blamed me for killing his brother and abandoned me in Moscow after clearly stating he didn't want to see me again.

I raised an eyebrow at him. Did he think I would forget all that because he decided he couldn't live without me after all?

"I'm sorry," he said. His face falling. "I should never have said what I did. Vaughn pointed out the error of my ways when he came to America and kicked my ass."

"You deserved it," I said, still unsatisfied, though interested in how that played out.

He nodded and licked his lips. "I was an idiot."

"A jerk face idiot," I said.

"Absolutely."

I narrowed my eyes at him.

A scratching sound, made me turn around. Singh was at the back door. Vincent stepped out and opened the door for the lion, who hopped in and turned around, parking his butt right on Alex. I laughed as the vampire moaned and tried unsuccessfully to move the lion off his lap. Singh looked at me and curled his lips into a weird lion smile. It was disturbing, but I appreciated the sentiment.

Vincent climbed behind the wheel again and started the engine.

I watched him as he pulled the vehicle onto the road and accelerated. His profile was strong, his jaw set as he focused on piloting us wherever we were going.

"Did Vaughn really beat you up?" I asked. Imagining it in my head made me giggle, and he turned to look at me with a goofy grin. It was strange on his face like it didn't quite belong.

"He kicked my ass. Trevor had to stop him, or I think he might have done permanent damage."

"Trevor stopped him?" I asked.

"Yeah, he is getting strong, but I think it was more shock that stopped my brother. Trevor is so small; when he grabbed my brother's arm and yelled, it was like a child telling his parents to stop fighting."

I pushed the thought of a child away and went back to imagining shy Trevor stopping the two old vampires in their tracks.

"I forgot to call him back," I said.

"Who? Trevor?" Vincent asked.

"Yeah. I called him whatever day that was and said I would call back because the reception was bad."

I caught Vincent's grin before he smoothed out his face.

"What?"

"It's nothing. You can talk to him when we get back to Narayan's house."

I nodded.

As the car entered Jaisalmer, the sounds of horns honking and the now familiar sight of camels and cows wandering the streets greeted us. Vincent piloted the small jeep through the narrow streets of golden sand buildings and through the narrow gate into the fort. He parked the car, and we all got out. Alex fell out when Singh finally hopped off him, and we made our way through the crowds towards the Lord of the city's house.

"Lark!" I heard and whipped my head up to find Trevor racing down the steps towards me. He flung his arms around my neck and clung like a monkey.

"What are you doing here?" I asked, hanging on to him for dear life.

"I came to help. I was worried about you." He finally let stood back so I could get a look at him. He had filled out since I had last seen him.

"Holy crap. You look great," I said.

"Thanks, come on. You need rest." He took my hand and led me past everyone and into the house. Singh bound past us and into the bedroom we had been using.

"Lark." I turned to find Nara, his head down. "I'm so sorry."

"It's not your fault," I said, though it kind of was. He shouldn't have been keeping those vampires. The rest wasn't his fault though.

"Thank you, Goddess."

I turned to follow Singh and Trevor, but Nara spoke again.

"My man from the south has brought word of Mahishasura."

My blood went cold.

CHAPTER SIX

I turned back to the vampire. "He has found Mahishasura?"

"Just stories. He heard a tale of a bison burning villages in the area of the caves."

"What caves?" Please don't let this jerk be underground again.

"Ellora caves," Vincent said from behind me. "It's a tourist site, but 90% of the caves are off limits. I was going to wait until you had eaten and rested before I told you." Vincent glared at Nara.

"Ok, well, I can hear about this while I get rest and food, right?" I raised an eyebrow at my bossy vampire.

"I'll have food brought to your room," Nara said, spinning on his heel.

"Be nice to him. He is a good man," I said as Vincent, and I walked down the hall to where Trevor and Singh were waiting.

Vincent raised an eyebrow at me but wisely kept his mouth shut. I was not taking any of his crap. I walked into the room to find Trevor and Singh flaked out on the bed. I made Trevor laugh by jumping over him to flop down on the bed between them. We were just missing Drew, and I felt bad for leaving him behind in Moscow. I remembered his face when I told him he wasn't coming with me.

I sighed and closed my eyes for a minute. I would have to apologize to him. I opened my eyes and propped myself up on the pillows so I could see Vincent. He sat on a chair in the corner, and I almost laughed. It was a wing-backed armchair, and he sat with a bland look on his face, like a king on a throne.

"Hey, are you a king?" I asked. "Everyone kept asking me about the king."

"I don't feel like a king. I think it might be like when you and Durga first began. Like he is there but not. Sometimes I feel something churning."

I laughed at the perplexed look on his face. "Oh, man, this will be crazy. I wonder if that's why Durga has been so quiet since you showed up." I sought the deity, and she stirred but didn't rise. Interesting.

My eyes locked on Vincent's. His glowing eyes faded to blue and my heart melted. "Do you feel that?" I asked, holding my breath.

"I've changed," he replied.

"No, nothing changed. You are still you, only now you share with someone else. Just like I do."

He nodded, and his eyes shifted back.

I took a deep breath. "OK, tell me about the buffalo man and the caves."

"In the south, there is an old monastery temple carved deep into the rock. No one knows how deep the caves go because most of the access points are too narrow for an adult to walk through. Many more they have barred off for generations to keep tourists from getting lost down there.

"We need to go there," I said. It wasn't a question.

Vincent nodded.

Trevor grabbed my hand. "Do you have to go now? You could stay for a bit," he said.

"Maybe tomorrow," I said. I wasn't feeling up to travelling across the country.

"I have a plane on standby," Vincent said.

"A big plane?" I asked.

"No."

Shit.

A woman walked in carrying a tray of food. She smiled at me and then set the tray on the bed.

"Thank you," I said as she hurried back out of the room.

Trevor and I dug into the food, and I flicked on the TV, handing him the remote so he could find something for us to watch.

That's how we ended up curled together between Singh and Vincent holding hands and screaming like girls at the scary movie he chose. Vincent rolled his eyes but smiled, and Singh slept through it, like usual. When the movie was over, we collapsed in giggles.

"All right, you've had your turn. I want time with Lark too," Vincent said, scooping me up off the bed and carrying me away.

"I'll talk to you in the morning before I leave," I said to Trevor who settled down with Singh. I reached out and flicked off the light as Vincent carried me through the doorway. He set my feet on the ground and took my hand, leading me to another door further down the hall.

He opened the door and ushered me in, but didn't turn on the light. The moon shone through the open doors of the balcony. This room was a mirror of the other, but the mood here was more serious and immediate. Vincent faced me, his arm sliding around my back and settling low on my spine. At the same time, his other hand cupped my neck and pulled me against him. I slid my hands up his chest and wrapped them around his neck. I had missed him so much in the desert, no matter how much I yelled that I didn't. I loved him.

He dropped his head and sealed his lips to mine, pressing and begging me for entrance with his tongue. I opened my mouth, and his tongue flicked against mine, making my heart race. The smell of his aftershave surrounded me like hot steam, raising my temperature and threading my pulse with his.

His hand behind my neck slid to my hip, and he lifted me off the floor. My legs slid around his hips, giving me a higher vantage point. I raised my hands to the sides of his head as he strode to the bed.

"Oh, god," I said.

His mouth was at my throat, his lips and teeth nipping at the sensitive skin and doing crazy things to my insides.

He laid me down on my back, covering me with his towering frame. He was a few degrees cooler than I was, making me feel like I had a fever. His hands caressed my body as his mouth licked my neck.

"Bite me," I said on a breathy voice.

I felt the sharp prick of his teeth, and then ecstasy flowed through my veins, relaxing every muscle in my body. I arched my back, and he licked my neck, closing the twin puncture there.

The night wore on as we got lost in each other.

"I love you," he whispered as I rested in his arms beneath the blankets. The sun was rising out the window.

"I love you too, Vincent." I figured if Durga killed me now, I would die happy. She could take her rules and fuck off. I could love this man and still fight her war. I could and I would. Durga pushed at me. I sat up, but she didn't want me to go anywhere, she had something but was asking to talk instead of forcing her way out. It was weird.

"What is it?"

"Durga has something to say."

"OK," he said, sitting up too.

Durga rose and the early morning sun shone red as my eyes shifted. Vincent's eyes changed from pink to purple, making him look even more beautiful than normal.

"I beg of you. Please do not hide her away. I will not interfere. That doesn't work anyway, but please, I must do my work."

"I would never stop her from doing what she wants. I have never stopped her from fighting the battles," Vincent said. He reached out and touched my cheek.

"Let me keep her. That is all I ask."

Durga slid back into her place inside me, leaving me free to do what I wanted. Vincent's eyes slid back to their usual vampire glow, but before they did, I memorized the exact shade of blue. They were brighter than Elliot's sky-blue eyes.

I reached out and ran my fingers across his stubbled cheek. "What colour were your eyes before you became a vampire?"

"My brother tells me we all had light blue eyes. It was our mother's eyes." He smiled, and my heart melted.

I wanted to tell him about Elliot, but it was way too soon to talk about kids. Could vampires even have kids? I bit my lip.

"What are you thinking about?" he asked, sitting up on an elbow.

I slapped a smile on my face. "I can tell you later." I leaned in to kiss him again, but he stopped me with a laugh.

"Tell me first."

I bit my lip again and tried to decide if I should tell him or not.

"Please?"

"The witch in the tunnel showed me a vision," I said hesitantly.

"What kind of vision?" he leaned back on the bed and tucked one hand behind his head. His chest was bare and the morning sun glinted off him, making him look like he was a God.

"There was a little boy."

"Uhuh?"

I chewed on my fingernail and studied him for another moment. He lay there blinking at me. I knew he could stay like that for as long as I could. Damn vampire. Finally, I shook my head and just spit it out.

"He was our little boy. He looked just like you."

He looked stunned. His eyes wide and staring at me as if I had just told him the river was on fire.

"Um, Lark," he said cautiously. "Vampires can't reproduce."

I looked away from him and let the sunrise burn my eyes. I wanted to take back the last five minutes. When he hadn't said that, I had hope. As tears stung my eyes, I pushed them back down and took a deep breath. Then I rose and started across the room towards the bathroom. A shower and some food and I would forget all about this conversation, go hunt down the bad guy and go home.

Maybe I could rebuild my yoga studio and get a cat. I could get a few cats. Vampires weren't allergic to cats. I was too young to worry about children, anyway. This was foolish.

"Lark." Vincent's arms wrapped around me and his body slid against mine until I buried my face in his chest and his arms held me together. He loaned me the strength I lacked as I fell apart.

"I'm so sorry," he whispered over and over as sobs shook me. Stupid crying. I needed to stop. I pushed him away and passed him, going into the bathroom and closing the door. I flicked on the light and the shower. The bathroom was beautiful with ceramic tile everywhere and tall brass taps. I stared at myself in the mirror. My hair was a mess after the night Vincent, and I had. My eyes were red and swollen. Fuck. I needed to get it together. I didn't want to be this girl. I asked Durga to take it away like I had a hundred times in the desert, but she ignored my plea. Instead, I played back my memories of the sweet boy in my dreams. I was such a masochist. I told myself I could adopt a little boy if I wanted, just as soon as this business with Mahishasura was over.

Steeling my resolve, I had a shower and tamed my wild hair. I dried myself off and wrapped up in a thick bathrobe. I wandered out determined to find everyone and make a plan of attack. I wanted to kill the stupid buffalo.

That is how I would get through. I had the man I loved, what more could I possibly need?

I told the little voice in my head to shut up. It was fighting time.

CHAPTER SEVEN

In the dining room with the long wooden table, I found Nara and several of his vampires. Vincent was also there as were Trevor, Singh and the female vampire who had fought with me against the fallen vampires in the city, Peri.

She smiled and waved at me. "You look pretty again," she said, and I laughed with her. I sat between her and Vincent and dug into some breakfast as soon as they set it in front of me. I was starving and needed to fuel up if I was going after the stupid buffalo.

Everyone was talking and discussing strategy and logistics about travelling. I looked over at Peri and winked. "Do you want to come fight a demon with me?" I asked her with a mouth full of flatbread thing with yummy spread stuff on it.

"Absolutely," she said. I gave her a thumbs up and stuffed more food in my mouth. They were still discussing things like airports and rental vehicles.

I chewed quickly and took a sip of the mug of coffee sitting in front of me. "I'm driving. No way am I getting on a small plane. Forget it."

Everyone stared at me like I was crazy and maybe I was.

"It will take days to get there by car," Vincent tried to mansplain to me.

"I don't care. Peri and I are gonna hit the road like Thelma and Louise." Peri laughed. Nobody else did. At least someone thought I was funny.

"Has she been drinking?" Trevor asked.

"I have not been drinking. But it would take more than desert moonshine to get me in one of those tin cans. We can take turns, drive all night and get there in no time."

Everyone still looked doubtful. I rose slowly to my full height which wasn't much, but they were all still sitting. Durga helped by turning my eyes red, and I spoke slowly, so there was no mistake. "This is my show. I will do as I please!" I punctuated it by slamming my hand down on the table. Everyone jumped except Singh who curled his lips in that weird lion smile thing he did before he went back to licking his plate. I looked around the room, pausing at every pair of eyes for a moment to the soundtrack of Singh's rough tongue removing the glaze from the ceramic plate they had served him on.

A round of "Yes, Durags" later, I pulled my chair back in and used a napkin to sop up the coffee I had accidentally spilled in the name of dramatic effect. Shit. I glanced at Peri who bit her lip so she wouldn't laugh and I gave her another wink. She might be the best friend I ever had. She liked killing vampires and getting bloody, and she wanted to drive across the country with me.

"Road trip," I whispered. She grinned and did a tiny happy dance in her seat. Yup. She was mine.

That reminded me. "Where is Drew?" I asked Vincent.

"He is in America. Helping Vlad with the city while I'm gone."

I nodded, then chugged my coffee and went to find clothes.

"I would like to come with you," Vincent said from behind me as I rifled through the closet of women's clothes in my size.

"You can fly if you would rather. I wouldn't mind getting to know Peri better. She fought with me, you know. She's funny and good with a blade."

"Are you pushing me away?" he asked, his eyes avoiding my gaze.

I backed out of the closet.

"Are you insecure now? I didn't know you had an insecure bone in your body," I teased as I approached him. I kept walking until I pressed my body up against his. I slid my hands around his waist and wove my fingers together locking him in place.

His eyes landed on mine. "I wasn't insecure until I met you. I've never made so many mistakes with someone in my life. It's like I can't see straight when I'm around you."

He dipped his head and caught my lips with his. He relaxed wrapping his arms around me. I hummed in his mouth, and he lifted me off the floor. My legs wrapped around his waist before he turned around and pressed my back into the wall, trapping me against his body.

He broke away and took a few heavy breaths before he spoke again. "I don't want to lose you again." He rested his forehead against mine.

"You won't," I said.

He kissed my forehead before setting my feet on the floor and taking a deep breath.

"Ok, we will fly out in the morning and meet you two at the Aurangabad Airport. It's south of the caves, so we can meet up and go together. Promise you won't go in alone?"

"You know you can't fight Mahishasura, right? Only Durga can."

"I know, but I want to be there when you face him. If he has a lot of rogues around, I can help. I'll bring some of Nara's men. Plus, I have a score to settle, and I want to see it done."

I patted his chest. "OK, we will see you there."

I walked past him and grabbed clothes, changing quickly. I grabbed a few extra sets of clothes, just in case, and headed out to find my road trip buddy.

Vincent found us a nice rental. It was a new car, and I suspected he purchased it off the lot, but let him tell me it was a rental, anyway. He had a thing about cars. It was a nineteen-hour drive to Aurangabad from Jaisalmer, so we would arrive in the morning.

The nice lady who always fed us packed a basket of food and snacks. Peri had driven south before so knew all the best places to stop if we needed to. I was sure we would at least need to stop for a bathroom break because I drank another cup of coffee before we left the house.

"Farewell, Lark. I hope we meet someday again," Nara said as I threw my extra clothes in the back seat of the car.

"I'm sure we will," I said with a smile and hugged him. As he pulled away, he took my hand and kissed the big ruby ring he gave me. Vincent glared but didn't rip Nara's head off, so that was nice.

While I had my back turned, human Singh slid into the back seat of the car.

"You can't take the plane?" I asked.

"Nope, I'm coming with you. I will stay a people, so I don't scare truck drivers."

"You will stay a people?" I asked.

He nodded, and I laughed at the ridiculous lion. I gave him two hours before he was itching to shift.

Vincent grabbed me up and kissed me hard. I laughed as he set my feet back on the ground. Then I got in the passenger seat. Peri had called first dibs on driving the new car. I let her, hoping she might dent it and teach Vincent a lesson about the value of old cars.

The car ran silently and slipped through the city like a ghost. I fiddled with the radio station until we were on the highway and I gave up on finding an English channel. The car radio had satellite, but I couldn't figure out how to switch it over, so I turned it off.

"Thank god," Singh said from the back seat.

"So, what do you do for fun, Peri?"

She smiled at me. "Hunt vampires and watch movies, mostly."

"Have you ever done yoga?" I asked.

"I have. I lived with a yogi in Tibet for a decade."

"Yes! I knew it. We need to do yoga together. I had a studio, but it got blown up," I said.

"You aren't very old to have had so much stuff happen to you."

I laughed. "How old are you?"

"I'm 462."

"Holy crap," I replied.

Singh huffed in the backseat, and I turned around to find he was a lion. Already. "You didn't even make it an hour in human form? What happened to 'I'll stay a people?' You will scare truck drivers."

He set his head back down on the seat and closed his eyes.

Peri was laughing from the driver's seat which made me laugh too. God, life was weird.

When our laughter died, I continued my questions.

"So how did you end up living here?" I asked as she switched lanes and passed a truck full of goats.

"I was travelling the world and fell in love with India. I've been here a long time. The magic is kind of gone, but I wasn't sure where I wanted to go." She glanced at me before looking back to the road. "When we kill this demon, I'd like to talk to Vincent about moving back to the US."

"That would be awesome. He can always use good fighters. I want to travel for fun, someday — not because some monster is killing people."

"I can understand that. I like fighting though, so I'm glad you are here. It's been boring the last hundred years."

"Glad to be of service," I said with a laugh.

We settled into a comfortable silence for a while. I watched the country go by out the window. It was mostly sand and scrub brush with the occasional wispy tree.

We switched at the first rest stop, and I took over the driving. It was awkward to drive on the wrong side of the road, but soon the desert gave way to more grass and shrubs. There were busses and cargo vans along with dirt bikes all vying for road space. People walked along the highway with goats. There were small tractors and the occasional cow roaming lose. I imagined hitting one would do some serious damage, but people here drove fast, and I loved it. The road was new and smooth.

Between the other drivers' speed and the open land, it didn't feel like I was going one hundred and thirty.

I slowed as we approached a small town. People and cows roamed the crowded streets. Motorbikes lined up in front of square buildings and goats running around. The center of the road had a cement partition in places or just a fence. I wasn't sure if it was to discourage cow crossing or pedestrian, but both were in ample supply. I coasted through and was nearly to the other side when Durga made herself known. She had been quiet since I came back from near dead or whatever I was. I slammed on the brakes and skidded to a halt on the narrow shoulder. Cars honked behind me and tires screamed on the hot pavement, but I had already unbuckled my seatbelt and thrown my door open.

"Yes!" Peri cried as she jumped out of her seat and skidded around the car to follow me.

She reached in and grabbed the keys, locking the car as I moved silently towards an old shed. It was rundown, and the door was half hanging off. Durga didn't push me to run, but she wanted me to go in the shed; it was curiosity.

As I approached, I realized someone chained the shed door closed. Wrapped through holes drilled in the steel door and padlocked was a thick chain. Rust ran across the lock as if no one had opened it in a while. I reached out hesitantly to touch the lock, but Durga lost patience and made me grab it and pull. Apparently, we were The Hulk now because the chain broke and the door swung open.

"Oh shit," I said taking a step backwards. There, in the dark, sat a vampire. He was gaunt like the ones in Nara's dungeon, but he also had his fangs removed. His mouth had two gaping black holes. Someone had chained him by the neck to the back wall, and it was the only thing holding him upright.

"That's disgusting," Peri said as she unsheathed her blade.

"Wait," I said. Durga rose and looked at the vampire. He was pathetic, and Durga felt sympathy for him. Not hatred or disdain like she had for the fallen rogue vampires in Jaisalmer.

The vampire's eyes remained locked on me with a plea for help. I think he would have begged if he had been able to move.

I stepped into the darkened shed and squatted down in front of the man. He didn't snap his teeth or try to bite me. He wasn't even fallen. He had been in here god knew how long and kept his sanity and humanity? I reached out and pulled the chain around his neck, breaking the heavy links. He hit the ground with a thud, and the chain rattled and clanked against the steel wall.

Durga reached out to touch the man's face. His sunken cheek was cold under my fingertips. I wanted to ask him his name, but I knew he couldn't speak. I could see now that his clothes were bloodstained and torn as though someone had beaten him. Durga warmed my fingertips. "I'm sorry, this will help."

As my hand grew hotter and hotter, the man's eyes grew wide, and his mouth opened slightly wider in a silent scream. A single bloody tear sprung to his eye, it was thick like sour milk. I watched it ran slowly down his face as the pain of the fire burned away the damage that someone had done to him. He gasped a breath and closed his mouth. His hand rose to cover mine on his cheek, and he tipped his head into my palm. He blinked away the last of his tear and sighed.

"Thank you, Goddess." His voice scratched like an old record.

"Who has done this to you?"

"It was the demon." The voice sounded familiar now, but I couldn't place it. It was someone I knew.

"I will slay him."

"Of course, you will." The vampire's lips curled up into a terrifying smile, and I finally recognized him as

Ninel. Little of his appearance remained. If not for the curve of his smile, I would not have figured it out.

"Where is Vilen?" she asked

"He remained behind, Goddess, to continue your work in Moscow."

"Very well. You need a good meal and rest before you are fit. Come, I will find you a willing sacrifice unless you rather end your journey in this world. I have learned it is not wise to force those who do not wish to continue to do so."

It felt like Durga was talking to me.

"No, Goddess. I have much left to do in service to you, but I would not wish to slow you down. Leave me and continue. I will not be fit for some time after the damage the demon has inflicted."

"I have a few moments to spare. Also, you are good company for my travels. Lark and her new friends are tiresome."

I tried to object, but Durga was in full control at this point, so I put it in the memory bank to discuss next time we were chatting.

Durga rose and pulled Ninel to his feet. Holding him upright and slinging his arm around my neck, she finally let go of control and let me navigate Ninel to the car. Singh was snoring in the back seat. Lazy lion. I swung open the door and gave his furry butt a boot; he grumbled and shoved over enough that Ninel could sit on the seat.

I slipped into the driver's seat and waited for Peri.

"How do you guys get blood, anyway?" I asked.

She chuckled. "How long have you been living with vampires?"

"Well, I haven't asked about the blood drinking thing." I remembered Vincent biting me the night before, and my heart kicked up a notch. I understood why someone would want to let a vampire bite them now though.

Peri gave me a wicked grin. "Come, I will teach you the ways of my people," she said in a deep voice. I laughed, but got back out of the car and hit the door lock button, so nobody messed with my car. There was still a lion in the backseat so I doubted anyone would open the door.

My loose pants and top flapped in the wind like a flag as we walked back into the small town. The large trucks driving through barely slowed, but traffic came to a standstill up ahead when a cow wandered on to the road. There was a car honking its horn and edging closer to the animal, but the animal didn't hurry. It was a badass cow.

Peri grabbed my sleeve to get my attention as she turned between some dirt bikes and headed for a small door. The building was sand coloured like most were, but the door was turquoise.

I tried to keep watching the cow but had to assume he made it safely across the road as I entered the building and lost sight of my new spirit animal.

Inside were tables and chairs set up like a diner. The ceiling was a pinwheel with spokes coming from the center of the room and meeting the walls. They had strung colourful ribbon between the spokes making it look more like a carnival than a diner.

Some people sat around in small groups, chatting quietly, drinks in their hands. I realized it was a bar. I was driving so I definitely couldn't order here, but Peri strutted up to the counter and ordered something. She spoke smoothly, and the man behind the counter smiled at her. She put money on the counter and as soon as he set down the drink; she slung it back. Then she winked at the man and gave him a come-hither kind of look. She stopped to look back and smile at him before walking out the door.

"Three, two..." she started counting.

A man came running up behind us. He stared at Peri like she invented chocolate. She reached out and took his hand, leading him back to the car. She pushed him up against the back bumper and pressed herself into him. Her mouth traced the line of his neck, and he tipped his head back.

It was awkward for them to be making out here by the side of the road, but the man didn't seem to mind. I stood and watched for a few moments until Peri's teeth broke his skin. The man's body trembled, and he went limp. She looked at me and motioned her head towards the car. Right, Ninel.

I unlocked the car and pulled the sleepy vampire out. He was still unsteady.

"He doesn't have teeth," I whispered. The man pressed against the car smiled. He was in some kind of trance or something.

"I'll open the vein, you hold your friend up here next to my buddy," she said smiling at me with blood-stained teeth.

I propped Ninel up, and he turned his head to look at our victim.

Peri bit the man's neck again, and this time when she pulled away, blood sprayed out. Two solid pumps shot across the ground before Ninel slammed his mouth down on the open vein and I watched his throat bobbed. You could feel the relief coming from Ninel as the blood rushed out. A few moments later, Ninel's tongue slid up the man's neck, and the blood stopped.

"This is how you make road trip memories," I said, stuck between horrified and intrigued.

CHAPTER EIGHT

"Our first memory together. Awe. We are bff's now," Peri said.

I broke out in giggles. It wasn't our first, though. When she mocked me for my face injury was the best memory. I wasn't sure why I guess it made me feel normal.

"I might have a bit of girl crush on you, Peri."

She broke down laughing too. I wedged Ninel back in beside the lion while Peri sent the human on his way.

"Won't he remember being bitten?" I asked.

"Some do, but there is no evidence of injury, so they assume it was a fun make-out session with a stranger. Call girls are great too. They don't ask questions."

"You bite call-girls?" I asked shocked.

"Yup. They don't care as long as someone pays them."

I pulled on to the highway and put my foot down. Our little diversion would make us late if I didn't hustle.

"So, are you and Vincent together?" Peri asked breaking the silence.

"I guess so. We haven't talked about it, but he said he loves me," I said. I slowed for a truck blocking half the road. When the oncoming traffic had passed, I sped up and passed him easily.

"Vincent seems kind of like a jerk," Peri said. I snorted a laugh. "Yeah, maybe. But most of the time he is sweet, and he believes in me. I don't think anyone has ever believed in my ability the way he does. It's a confidence boost."

"I could see that. I had to fight my way into the ranks and then up them. Old vampires are a boys' club."

"That is so true," I said.

"What is it like to have Durga inside you?" she asked.

"It's kind of like having a roommate. She breaks all my stuff and screws up my life and doesn't pay rent."

Peri laughed, and I joined her. It was weird, but I was used to Durga now.

By the time we reached the next rest stop, Ninel was sitting up in the back seat. He was right, though, it would take more than a little blood to fix whatever had happened to him.

"Why did you come here, Ninel?" I asked as I waited for Peri to come back with some road snacks. The gas tank was full, and I switched to the passenger seat.

"I came to find you. When you left, I thought you would call for me, but then you disappeared and didn't answer your phone. I feared you were in danger."

"How long were you in there?"

"What day is it?"

"The 17th," I said and realized it was my birthday tomorrow. Happy birthday to me. Time to crawl around in some caves and kill a buffalo man.

"I was in there for two weeks. It felt much longer. His vampires drained me."

"He has vampires again?" Great, I love hordes of fallen rabid vampires.

"Yes, I'm afraid he has quite a few."

Ninel's eyes were sliding shut, so I stopped asking him questions and let him rest.

The driver's door opened, and Peri slipped in with two shopping bags. She passed them over and started the engine.

"Did you buy the whole store?" I asked.

"I didn't know what you liked," she said absently as she spun the tires on the gravel and got us out on the highway before a transport truck.

It was a hodgepodge of western and local foods and snacks. They had chips in the same brands as at home, but different flavours. I popped one bag open and bit into the chip. It tasted like the food they had severed me in the desert -- spicy and savoury.

"We don't have this kind in America," I mumbled before shoving another chip in my mouth.

We drove for several more hours before switching again. It was dark now. If it weren't for the fact that traffic was almost non-existent and I could use my high beams, I definitely would have hit a few cows. Did cows not sleep? Singh and Ninel were both silent, and when I looked over at Peri, she had closed her eyes too. I knew vampires didn't sleep, but I had seen Drew do this before. Just close his eyes like he was asleep.

I pulled into a rest stop and killed the engine. It was still dark, but I needed something else to eat.

"You want me to come with you?" Peri asked, her eyes flashing in the moonlight.

"Nah, I'll just be a sec."

Singh roused himself enough to yawn.

"You want something?" I asked him.

He licked his lips. I would assume that was lion for "yes, please."

As I approached the small store, a figure pulled out of the shadows. I stopped dead, ready to kick ass. It wasn't until the figure stepped out into the light cast from the window of the store, I realized she wasn't a fallen or rogue vampire.

"Are you her?" the woman asked. Her tiny hand reached out as if I was an aberration and she could reach right through me. When her hand met my shoulder, she yanked it back as if I had burned her.

"It's true. You have returned."

"Who are you?" I asked. She had a look of awe on her face, so I dropped my defences.

"My name is Darri. I have been waiting for you, Lark. The witch told me to wait here. She showed me your face and said I would find you someday and I had to give you a message."

A set of car headlights swept over the parking lot, and Darri shied away.

"What message?"

She took a step back into the shadows. "Wait."

"She said to tell you to give the lightning back to the king of thunder."

"What?" I stepped into the shadows, but no one was there. I took a few more steps and peered into the dark around the corner of the building. Durga lit the area in red, but it was no use, the woman had disappeared.

I turned back and collided with a figure behind me. I screamed, and then the other person screamed, and I realized it was Peri.

"What the hell?" she yelled.

"Shit, I'm sorry," I said. Then a laugh bubbled up. "You should have seen your face."

Peri tried to maintain her angry face, but couldn't hold it in. Her laughter spilled out, and we were both wiping the tears of laughter from our eyes as we entered the rest stop store.

I grabbed a bunch of snacks and some meat sticks for the lion, and then Peri helped me carry it all out to the car.

"Where are you putting all this food you are eating?"

"Hey, I walked through the desert for weeks, I'm just trying to catch up."

Peri drove the last leg of our trip, and I filed her in on the weird woman I had seen. Then I told the story of Alex and his "save the Lark, crown the king" words he got from some witch too. I was interested in meeting this witch with the visions. Witches didn't live forever though.

There was no way she was still alive.

I knew as we approached the Ellora caves. I could feel the evil in my bones. A deep-seated urge washed over me to jump out of the moving vehicle and face the buffalo bastard, but I restrained it. I promised Vincent, and I needed backup if the horned jerk had a bunch of rogues. I didn't doubt Durga could fight them off, but I needed to get Mahishasura locked in battle. He needed to be my only focus. Durga jumped and spun inside me. Her anger was all-consuming. She flashed on the backs of my eyelids when I blinked. Her arms waved with weapons; she was ready.

"Soon," I muttered to the impatient deity.

"What's that?" Peri asked.

"I was just telling Durga to keep her pants on."

"I'm ready for a good fight, too," she said, gripping the wheel.

As the sun came up, we approached a city. I was sure it was Aurangabad, and the guys would be here this morning. We had made excellent time though. Between Peri's lead foot and my own, we were three hours early.

"What do you want to do to kill 3 hours?" I asked her.

"I am so stiff. We should find a yoga studio," she said.

"That is a great idea." It had been too long since the last time I did yoga. I was sure my body was out of shape now.

We drove around the city as people were waking up and opening their shops. We couldn't find a studio, so we stopped at a small park in the middle of the city. It stood abandoned still at this early hour, so we picked a grassy spot facing the rising sun and went through the motions of sun salutations. The smooth movement and soft stretches of the warmup routine felt like coming home. I hadn't done yoga in months, and my body reminded me.

Its protests and snaps went unheeded as I continued through the movements. Sweeping my arms up, I stretched my body towards the sky. Then I shifted to the next position using my core muscles to keep my body in line. After a few minutes, I had a light sheen of sweat. Peri moved in time with me, like we had been doing yoga together for years. She was more limber than I was. She moved smoothly, and she paused in a more balanced frame. I wished I hadn't fallen so far away from my roots.

Yoga had been my life. Maybe it could be again when I finished taking care of Mahishasura.

Peri moved into more advanced movements, and I tried to keep up. Just as I thought I was about to fall, Durga offered me her strength. She flowed through my muscles and smoothed their movements, removing the burning sting of disuse.

"Thank you, Goddess," I whispered.

The feeling of being free and blessed flowed through me. I thanked her again in my mind, for not giving up on me in the desert. I promised her I would do better and be better. She remained silent, but I felt peace between us.

As I lay down in the soft sandy grass, my chest rising and falling in a deep, steady rhythm, my own sense of peace was all I could feel. I had made it through the storm, now safe on the shore. Thoughts of Elliot still lingered, but they didn't consume me. If I never got to know that sweet boy in life, I would see him when I died. I smiled up in the sun, my eyes closed against its harsh light and let the warmth of the day dry my skin.

"That was a great workout," Peri said.

I opened one eye and looked over at her. She was laying on her back too. "It was. I haven't been doing yoga as much as I should."

"I noticed you struggling. Lazy cow."

I tore up some grass and threw it at her; she laughed and brushed it off. "All right, let's get going, the guys should be at the airport in less than two hours. Plus, I want to eat something. I've been starving all night."

I stood up and held out my hand for Peri who accepted it, and we walked back to the car where the lazy bums were still resting.

Singh was snoring away. I was getting worried about how much he slept. Maybe he needed a healthier diet. One of his big paws was hugging an empty chip bag. Were chips even safe for lions?

Ninel's head had drooped to the side and propped on the window, but his chest rose and fell in a steady rhythm. Peri got into the driver's seat, and we crossed the city towards the airport. It was easy to find as planes landed and took off from the west side of the city.

"STOP!" I yelled, waking everyone in the backseat and nearly causing an accident as Peri swerved. Horns honked, and Peri cursed.

"What the hell, Lark?" Peri shouted.

"McDonald's!!" I pointed and bounced in my seat. Those beautiful golden arches lit up the early morning like a lighthouse, and I was a ship lost at sea.

Peri gave me an "oh my god, you're crazy" look, but turned on her turn indicator.

I put my window down and could smell the greasy reminder of home. I almost fainted I inhaled so hard. It wasn't right, but it was close. There was a distinct spice smell of customary Indian food, but it was still McDonald's.

Peri pulled the car up to the drive-through window; they didn't have a speaker. The menu was familiar and right there in a colour photo was a sausage and egg McMuffin. Holy glory.

"Hi," I said to the woman in the window. I would like ten sausage and egg McMuffins and ten hash browns, please. Also, an apple juice."

The woman tapped it into the cash register, and I looked back at Singh. "Do you want anything?"

Singh's eyes opened and closed again. I would take that as a no. When I looked back at the woman in the window, her disinterested face had morphed into shock at the sight of my white lion. Right.

Peri handed the woman a credit card, and after a moment she reached out and took it, her eyes dancing between the window and the machine to swipe the card.

Peri nearly had to climb in the window to get her card back as the woman wouldn't reach back out.

A few minutes later I was holding a bag of greasy heaven in my arms. I stuffed one sandwich in my mouth, and my taste buds went into overdrive. I moaned, and Peri laughed at me, but I didn't care. Even with all the food I stuffed into me while we drove, nothing filled my stomach like good old fried food.

When we pulled into the airport parking lot, I left Singh and Ninel behind again, parking in the farthest part of the lot, so they were under the shade of a tree. I left the windows cracked. They were probably fine.

Peri and I walked into the bustling airport. It was like a shiny warehouse with big pillars holding up the roof. Skylights let in natural light, and they had built round gardens into the floor. Their flowers and shrubs added an earthy feel to the steel and glass interior.

Travellers hustled in and out pushing carts stacked with luggage or dragging suitcases behind them. We followed signs for arrivals and just as the crowd cleared; I saw the back of a tall blond-haired man. I froze. As he turned around, his eyes lit on mine. His lips curled up into a wicked grin that sent dimples to his cheeks and sparkles to his glowing eyes.

My heart and my stomach did a funny little flip, and a moment later I was in his arms.

CHAPTER NINE

"God you two, get a room," Peri said as I broke the kiss with Vincent. He was just so yummy. I gave Peri the finger and Vincent another quick kiss before he set my feet on the ground.

"You taste like bacon," he said with a laugh.

"I found a McDonald's!"

He chuckled and picked up his bag. "You two have a good road trip?"

"Yeah, we can talk about it somewhere else though. I have a few things you should know."

Vincent took my hand, but before I turned around, I saw freaking Alex standing at the luggage carousel.

"What is Alex doing here?" I said loud enough for most of the airport to hear me.

Alex spun around to look at me.

"He has to be here, Lark."

"That's crap. He should be hiding under a rock somewhere. We can't trust him," I glared at the vampire and then turned my back on him.

"I'm sorry, I feel like he needs to be here," Vincent said in a low tone. The apology wasn't entirely sincere. His eyes flashed blue for a moment, and it reminded me that he had a God riding him like I had Durga. Freaking Gods always had weird plans.

"Fine, but I will not trust him to have my back," I said.

"OK," Vincent said, kissing my forehead.

"Can we go kick ass now?" Peri asked, her hands on her hips and toe-tapping.

"Keep your panties on," I said. A dozen of Nara's guards had flow in with Vincent. They were a wall of muscle, each carrying a duffel bag. Vincent stopped at the rental car desk and picked up three sets of keys, handing them out to the guards.

"Can I ride with you?" He asked before he handed off the last set.

"My car is kind of full."

"Has Singh been a lion this whole time?" he asked.

"Yes, but I also picked up a hitchhiker." I thought about it for a moment. "I guess that's not funny. I found Ninel locked up in a shed, drained and beaten."

"I will ride with the crew," Peri said, cutting in and stealing the keys out of Vincent's hand. "You two can catch up on the drive to the caves." Her eyebrows waggled suggestively. Weirdo.

"Problem solved. I want to talk to you about something else that happened," I said, turning for the doors.

Once we were outside, Vincent took my hand and walked with me to the car parked at the back of the lot. The sun had moved, but it was still mostly in the shade. I got in the driver's seat and started the engine and the air conditioning. Singh was panting. His pink bristly tongue was curled and sticking out of his open mouth. He narrowed his eyes at me.

"You could have opened the door if you had turned back into a person for half a second," I reminded him.

Vincent slid into the passenger side and turned to look at the vampire and lion in the back seat. "Shit," he muttered. "I can't believe that's Ninel."

"I didn't recognize him at first. Mahishasura's gang of fallen vampires took a round or two out of him."

"My Goddess has already healed me a bit," he said, his mouth still empty of fangs. I wasn't sure that Durga had done anything. He didn't look better.

"You rest, Ninel. When this is over, we can get you more blood and back on your feet."

Ninel nodded and then tipped his head back like it was too heavy.

"There is something else," I said when Vincent turned back around.

"What is it?"

"I met a woman at a rest stop. She said a witch sent her to meet me. I'm not sure if it's the same witch as Alex, but how many witches are likely to do that? The woman said to give the king of thunder the lightning."

"What does that mean?" Vincent asked.

I opened my mouth to reply, But Durga rose suddenly and took over. My vision turned red, and Vincent's eyes changed from normal to purple. I was not going to get used to that.

"Indra, it is good to see you again," Durga said.

"Goddess, I have been busy, but now I have come to assist you in this final leg of your battle."

"Very well. Let us get to work then."

Indra nodded, and Durga receded, leaving me staring into the blue eyes of a God.

"I have made a few minor adjustments to your mate."

"What kind of adjustments."

The God who was using Vincent's body smiled. "A king must have an heir," he said before Vincent's eyes faded back to normal and we sat staring at each other for a long second.

"Uhm," I said.

"That was strange."

"OK, let's go then, shall we?" I asked, dropping the whole topic but starting a little argument with myself in my mind. If he meant I would have my baby, my Elliot, I was going to happy dance, but I didn't want to get my hopes up. Gods were annoyingly vague and tricky bastards. Shiva was proof of that. I couldn't imagine what else he could mean, but I put the car in reverse and pulled out of the parking space.

I didn't have space in my mind for anything except the upcoming fight with the monster. He had to die.

Vincent hit a few buttons on the radio and found not only an English station but the one from back home. It was so weird to hear the same DJ's I always listened to coming through the speakers in this foreign land. It made me even more homesick.

We made a quick stop at a motel, got a key and tucked Ninel into a bed to rest. Then I used my superior driving skills to get us out of the city at breakneck speeds.

We pulled up to the partially filled parking lot at the Ellora Caves and met up with the rest of the guys. They were all lined up like solider.

"Be cool, guys," I said. Peri repeated something in Marwari, and the men fell out of formation and took on a relaxed stance that worked. I mean, they didn't look like tourists, but they didn't look like an elite paramilitary squad. It was a good effort.

"Ok, we'll take a tour, but we will have to come back at nightfall. Most of the caves are off limits," I said.

Peri translated, and we were on our way. The first cave, right by the parking area, was a tall pillared building carved out of rock. The voices of all the visitors echoed through the high-ceilinged space. We walked up the steps and past a pair of what looked like walruses carved meticulously. As we got into this first cave, it got darker until we came out to a balcony that looked out over the rest of the caves. There were dozens, maybe hundreds here. Sculptures graced all the walls, some Gods I recognized and others Durga used my mouth to name out loud. The amazing work and the effort made to construct these caves was phenomenal. It wasn't a structure made of stone; it was a single stone chiselled into a temple. Earth still lay upon the top and as I looked out over the caves at a different site. You could see how the stone was once whole until generations of people worked to change them.

Durga pulled me away from this place. Mahishasura wasn't in these busy open caves. He was in another system altogether. Back out at the parking lot, there was a walkway from one set of caves to another, but it had eroded with time, and the guards blocked it off. A natural spring created a waterfall from the top of the cliff down to the ravine below, the spray creating a rainbow. It was almost magical. Durga pushed at me, and I turned back to the team. "We will have to drive around to the other side," I said.

This area was just as busy, and Durga was getting impatient. She would have to wait till nightfall. People and security guards filled the place. If we broke down a gate, someone would notice.

The second set of caves had carvings three stories high — gods made of stone to guard these holy places. We passed a security guard, and I made a note of the simple padlock that hung from the open wooden door of this cave. We passed through the building and into a courtyard of stone. A giant monument stood in the center on a raised platform, guarded by a stone elephant. His trunk had fallen off, but the rest of him remained. Beyond the elephant was a giant temple of stone.

"They carved this from a single rock. It's Shiva's temple," Peri explained.

"How do you know?" I asked, looking up at the three stories tall building.

Peri held up her cell phone with a website open. Oh.

Durga wanted to rush me, but I had to see it. I had been in Shiva's temple so many times, could this be the place I had visited?

Dozens of stone elephants stood to watch all around the base of the temple, their intricate faces crumbling, but still recognizable.

I followed a group of people and made my way inside the temple. It was beautiful and ornate, but nothing like Shiva's simple home. This had vaulted ceilings, decorative carvings, plus it was dark. I walked back out again, feeling disappointed. I wasn't sure why; it seemed a silly thing to get excited about, but I had been in a strange mood for days.

Vincent slung his arm over my shoulders, and we moved on.

The sheer volume of people visiting the caves was staggering. Every site and every cave was full of people. Peri pulled up more info on her phone and found a video of a guy who was explaining his theory of how they cut the stone. He believed it was aliens that carved the temples and caves in Ellora. He was convincing.

I tuned out the video and kept looking around. We had found a cave that was pretty much unoccupied by tourists, and I felt closer to the evil here. I sat on the sandy floor and took deep breaths. When my senses flooded out, my stomach sank. There had to be hundreds of vampires underground. The entire area lit up. I found Mahishasura too. He didn't have the witch to hide him, so he was easy to see. His light was brightest among the vampires in the underground caves. I watched for a while, hoping to see how they got in and out, but they didn't move around much.

I pulled my senses back in and opened my eyes. The team was all laughing and watching Peri's cell phone over her shoulder. I stood up and dusted off my pants. As I moved closer to the group, I recognized the story on the video they were watching. It was the story of Durga and Mahishasura told with cartoons for children. I had watched the same video and found it disappointing that the real Mahishasura wasn't an animated caricature when he appeared in front of me. In fact, there was nothing fun about the real buffalo demon. He was big and hairy and ugly.

"You ready to go, Lark?" Vincent asked over the noise of the chuckling soldiers.

They all straightened out and wiped the laughter from their faces, but Peri kept watching and laughing.

"Yeah, let's go. I have to find the entrance to the underground tunnels," I said. Then I thought about it and looked at all the guys who had been trailing along with us. "Let's divide into teams of three. Your job is to search every tunnel for any suspected entrance and make a note. Look for book scuffs or recently opened locked doors. Anything that looks like it could lead to an underground area."

The men quickly dispersed. Peri gave me a wave and wandered off with two guys. That left me alone with Vincent, Singh and friggin Alex.

"Can someone explain why this backstabber is here? He is probably reporting back to Mahishasura everything we are doing."

"How could I possibly do that, Lark? I told you that you had to be in that cage, but I knew you wouldn't be there long. Otherwise, everything would have happened differently, and things have to play out as they must. I can't change the future."

"How do you know? Maybe you should have killed that bastard. I could be sipping Mai Tai's on a tropical beach right now instead of digging in the sand looking for a stupid buffalo demon."

My stomach growled, dissolving the seriousness of my whole rant.

"I saw a food vendor in the parking lot," Alex said, hooking his thumb over his shoulder.

I scowled at him. "At least you are useful for something," I grumbled and stomped past the vampire, heading for the cave entrance.

Out at the parking lot, I found a man with a small cart and Vincent paid for a bowl of rice and naan for me. He and I sat in the shade of a small tree while I ate. Alex skulked about looking at the carved rocks that lay on the grass. The stones must have been test pieces or something for the ancient men who built the caves. Not all the temples were Hindu, some were Buddhist temples with other gods carved into the rock, and some were Jain origin. They numbered the caves since there was over 100 of them.

A soft breeze blew across the open area, kicking up sand. I shovelled the last of my spicy rice into my mouth and guzzled a bottle of water. Ready to get back at it.

"Lark, wait a minute," Vincent said as I went to stand up.

"What is it?"

"I wonder if you aren't being too harsh to Alex," he said.

"He locked me in a cage under Moscow."

"Yes, but he has explained that, and he saved you back in Jaisalmer."

I sighed. Damn it, why did I always have to be the bigger person? "Fine, I will stop being mean to the little vampire. But if he even hints at being a double-crossing liar again, I will slaughter him."

"I'll help," Vincent said. He leaned in and kissed me, and I forgot all about the weaselly little jerk. Vincent's arms came around me, and he pulled me into his lap, his lips never leaving mine. My empty rice bowl fell in the grass, but I couldn't care about littering at that moment.

"Thank you, Lark," Alex said, ruining the moment.

I pulled away from Vincent, collecting my garbage and hoping to my feet.

Time to get back to cave diving.

I sent out my senses and tracked the vampires above ground, ignoring the ones below. When I found a cave they weren't in, we headed that way. Hopefully, we would have this all checked out by nightfall. I wanted to kick vampire ass tonight.

We spent hours traipsing through sandy caves with intricate carvings of various gods but didn't find any with possible underground entries. We found many holes in the temple floors that could be for rain run-off; it rained occasionally. More likely, they were ventilation shafts for those underground caves we couldn't find our way to. As we exited the last cave, the sun was hanging low in the sky. Vincent's phone battery was nearly dead from being used as a flashlight for so long.

"Lark!" I heard a voice call. It echoed so I couldn't tell where it came from. I scanned the horizon and found someone that might have been Peri waving her arms like an air traffic controller.

We booked it up a path that led to another trail along the ridge of the rock to get to where she was.

"Hey, found something?" I asked as we approached.

"Yup," she smiled and rubbed her hands together.

We followed her to a cave entrance that was nearly invisible in the rock. A group of giant soldiers mulled about outside. Peri disappeared into the small crevice, so I followed behind her. It narrowed even more as we moved in until it was so tight, I had to turn sideways. I took tiny steps to squeeze through and was struggling to turn my foot when a hand grabbed my arm and yanked me through into an open space. Peri steadied me in the cavern. A few other people were standing holding flashlights.

"Lark," Vincent called from behind me. "I don't fit, Alex is coming through, don't kill him."

"Fine," I mumbled. Peri laughed and then yanked the skinny vampire through the gap harder than necessary. Making Alex yelp. Peri was definitely my BFF. She gave me a wicked grin like she could read my mind.

Alex straightened his shirt and dusted off his pants.

"So, this is not a great way to get in here if we can only get half the guys in," I said getting back to business.

"I agree, strategically it's bad for us unless we can lure most of the fallen out. That shouldn't be too difficult, but it would be better if we could sneak in here. I'm not too sure how it will work otherwise," she said.

The tunnel continued on a downward slope. I blocked everything out and sent out my senses — so many vampires. I wouldn't even be able to get past them to get to Mahishasura if they all came out at once.

"Ok, let's get out of here and discuss this. I don't want to alert them to our presence yet. We need a plan," I said. We all shimmied back through the narrow entrance. When I stumbled out the gap in the rock, Vincent was there to catch me.

The serious look on his face confirmed that he had heard us talking. We headed back towards the vehicles as the caves were closing soon. Our time was up.

"We need to get in there and get the majority of the fallen out so I can get through to Mahishasura. He is the farthest from that opening. All his little guards are surrounding him."

"Did someone order magic?" A voice behind me called. I spun around, and tears sprung to my eyes.

"Frankie!"

CHAPTER TEN

I flung myself at Frankie, and he caught me in his arms. "I missed you," I whispered.

He set me on my feet and smiled down at me. "I missed you too." His smile morphed to a curious look, but just as it registered, Vincent spoke.

"Thanks for coming, Frankie." Vincent extended a hand to the warlock, and they shook.

"Holy shit," Peri mumbled from behind me. I spun around to look at her. "Introduce me." Her voice was a low whisper her eyes on the hot warlock candy. Frankie was wearing his typical jeans and a tight t-shirt under his coven's leather jacket and the shit-kicking leather boots on his feet.

"Frankie," I said interrupting whatever he and Vincent were talking about. "I would like you to meet

Peri." I used my most formal voice to make it official that my new BFF met my oldest BFF.

"Nice to meet you," Frankie's brown eyes twinkled as he extended a hand to Peri. She set her fingers in his hand like she was a delicate flower. I almost laughed but managed to bite my lip and control it.

"Let's get out of here, and we can discuss strategy," Vincent said, ushering us all towards the vehicles. I led the procession of rental cars back to the city. Vincent used the last of his cell phone battery to call and reserve a few more rooms at the motel where we stashed Ninel. It was like no time had passed at all since I had last seen Frankie, but somehow it wasn't awkward like I expected it to be. Frankie seemed happy.

Every time I checked the rear-view mirror, he smiled at me from the back seat. I was glad he wasn't mad or upset, but it was kind of strange. We wove back through the city, and I pulled into the McDonald's drive-through. I didn't care if no one else wanted the greasy fast food. I was, once again, hungry. Everyone ordered food. Even Singh stayed human long enough to get his order in. Then we headed to the motel.

The rest of the vampire soldiers were already there. I pulled out the bags of food and carried them to the waiting group while Vincent scampered off to get the room keys.

"Did you get food for all of us Lark, or are all those for you?" Peri asked, a smirk on her face.

"Don't make fun of her," Frankie said as he walked past me to stand beside Peri. They looked cute together.

"Yeah, Peri. Don't make fun of me," I said, sticking my tongue out at my friend.

"She is eating for two, after all." Frankie laughed.

The smile fell from my face, and I dropped my bag of burgers on the gravel driveway. "That's not funny Frankie," I said as tears gathered in my eyes. My hands shook, and I reached down to pick up the bag. Luckily it hadn't spilled because no matter how much I had been trying to block out the thought of Elliot, the reminder did nothing to squelch my appetite.

"I assumed you knew," Frankie said. I dropped the bag again and stood up.

I swallowed hard. "I don't think this is funny," I warned him. A tear burst over my eyelid and rolled down my cheek. Silence had fallen on the group.

He stepped forward and cupped my face with his hands. "How could you not know?" Frankie said. I shook my head. I didn't know what he was saying.

"What's going on?" Vincent asked, striding up with violence in his eyes.

"You didn't tell her?" Frankie asked him.

"Tell her what?" Vincent asked his teeth bared as he took in the tears running down my face. Vincent's hands clamped into fists, and the rest of the vampires took a few steps back. Including Peri. Couldn't blame her.

"Listen, you idiot," Frankie said, turning back.

"No, you listen! What the hell have you done?" Vincent steamed. His eyes turned blue — the most beautiful blue I had ever seen.

"No, Vincent! Listen with your god damn ears!" Frankie's voice cut through the tension and Vincent's eyes fell on me. His anger melted and his eyes dropped to my stomach.

I opened my mouth to say something, but no words came out.

Vincent took a long stride towards me and fell to his knees wrapping his arms around my waist, pulling my stomach to his ear. Tears kept running down my cheeks. I looked around, and everyone was staring. Peri's mouth hung open.

A bird called and flew from the tree to land in the gravel. It hopped forward and looked up at me. Its fragile wings tucked against its body, its tiny eyes looked at me for a moment.

I put out my hand, and the little bird flew up to cling to my finger. It was so light, I almost couldn't feel it there. A light flutter in my stomach had me looking back down at Vincent. His blue eyes were red-rimmed and wet.

"It can't be," he whispered.

I felt another flutter in my stomach, and the small bird flapped its tiny wings. It hovered for a moment before it took to the sky and soared above us calling out into the night.

Vincent rose and picked me up. I still hadn't found any words. He carried me to a door and unlocked it, then kicked it closed behind him and set me down on the bed.

He climbed over me and put his ear to my stomach again.

I took several deep breaths and rested my hand in Vincent's soft hair. "What does it sound like?" I asked, my voice cracking at the end.

"Perfect," he whispered before he shifted. His lips found mine.

"Wait," I said, pushing him away. "Is this real? Am I awake?"

He smiled so wide his eyes danced and glittered, and his fangs flashed in the low light of the motel room.

"Yes." His lips recaptured mine. His body pressed me down into the mattress, and we stayed like that for a long time, entwined together. His lips devoured mine. Eventually, the scratching at the door escalated to a roar, and we broke away laughing. Our relationship would never be just the two of us. I rested my hand on my stomach. We would be a family with a ridiculous pet.

Vincent stood up and opened the door, letting the white lion in. Singh had my bag of food in his teeth and set it on the floor before he launched himself onto the bed, jumping over me. He collapsed in a heap beside me and set his big furry head gently on my stomach. After a moment the loudest purr I had ever heard range from the silly cat.

"That's my spot, lion," Vincent said. Singh just yawned at him and then rested his chin back on my stomach and closed his eyes.

"That baby has a hell of a bodyguard," Vincent said.

"Elliot," I whispered.

"Is that his name?"

I nodded and pet the giant cat that guarded my baby already. My baby. I stared at the ceiling. Would I fight Mahishasura with a baby inside me? That was ridiculous.

Durga rose so fast, one second, I was in bed in the motel room and the next I was sitting in front of Shiva.

"Hello ch..." Shiva paused, his eyes studying me. Durga appeared beside him a moment later, her arms flapping like she was in a hurricane.

"I give you your wish, and this is how you repay me? You must end Mahishasura. We must do this." She scowled at me.

Shiva raised his hands when I looked back to him as if to say he is not getting involved.

"I didn't say I wouldn't. I have to wonder if its really a safe place for a baby."

"Ah, that's what it is. I knew something was different about you," Shiva said smiling and petting his snake as it zipped around his neck like a noose.

"The demon's demise is the only thing you need focus on. What life will your child have if you allow the demon to run free? The world will perish!" Durga's anger was palpable.

"Ok, holy God, calm down. Your arms will fall off if you don't stop waving them like that."

"Oh shit," Shiva whispered.

Durga's face went red, and she screamed as she kicked me out of meditation.

* * *

The room spun for a second when I opened my eyes. Guess me and Elliot would slay a buffalo demon. I rested my hand low on my stomach. It was still flat, but I could feel a flutter. I was no expert on babies, but I was pretty sure I should not be able to feel him kick yet.

"Oh shit," I exclaimed.

"What is it?" Vincent asked from across the room where he sat staring at his phone.

"I know nothing about babies," I said.

Durga's angry face flashed on the back of my eyelids.

"Never mind, I can deal with that after we take care of this little demon problem," I said to pacify the ancient Deity.

Vincent crossed the room and knelt beside the bed. I would have dragged him onto it, but a pesky lion was occupying most of it.

"You are going to be an amazing mother, and I can't wait to meet our boy, but you are right, we have to take care of this little problem. You ready to discuss a plan?" Vincent smiled. "I've been eavesdropping on the Peri and Frankie in the next room. They seem to get along well. Also, they have a plan."

"Perfect," I said, hopping up from the bed. I had kicked my shoes off, so I pulled them back on and grabbed my bag of now-cold burgers on my way out the door. The lion, snoring softly, kept the bed warm for me.

I knocked and pushed open the wooden door of the next motel room in time to see Frankie and Peri jump apart like two teenagers caught kissing behind the bleachers. Interesting. I bit my lip and pretended I had seen nothing.

"Hey, guys. Any idea how we are getting into those tunnels?" I asked, nonchalantly.

"Lark. Yeah, we've come up with an idea that might work," Frankie said, his cheeks pink. He sat down at the small table where they had maps spread out. Someone had drawn on the exact location of the narrow entrance we found.

"If we start here, I can shift you into the first open area that Peri described. I can't take you further without seeing it first, or I might end up dropping us into solid stone which wouldn't be great. But if we sneak in and take a quick look before they come out, I can take you in."

"If all the soldiers set up here, we can lure the fallen with some of your blood. The soldiers can take care of them while we head in." Frankie finished by pointing to the tiny arrow on the map.

"Sounds good," I said.

"I would be happier if you weren't going in alone," Vincent said.

"I'll be with her," Frankie said.

"Yes, but you only have magic, you don't have fighting skills too," Vincent pointed out.

"I have defensive magic. I can protect her," Frankie countered in an equally indignant voice.

I slammed my hand down on the table, stopping the idiots from their argument. "I don't need protection. Durga is a bloodthirsty, crazy person right now. She's got this." That stopped the fighting before it began.

Peri leaned over and whispered "that was hot" in my ear. I shook my head at her but smiled, anyway. This is why she is my best friend.

"I'll go with you lark," a voice said from across the room. I hadn't even noticed the slimy little vampire sitting there. I remembered Vincent had asked me not to be so combative with Alex and bit my tongue.

"It's ok. I got this. I'm the only one who can fight the buffalo jerk, anyway."

"Actually," Peri interjected. "I can help. I'm a woman."

"Can you get Peri and I both in?" I asked Frankie.

Frankie nodded his eyes locked on Peri like he wanted to object to her going in. Awe. He was in for a rough ride if he tried to control Peri. I was sure that would go over like a lead balloon.

"All right, Peri and I can go fight the buffalo man, while all the rest of you kill fallen vampires.

"Slice and dice," Ninel said from the bed. I hadn't noticed him there either. I needed to pay more attention to my surroundings.

"You stay here and guard the fort, big guy," I said.

He nodded, and his eyes slid closed again. Maybe he would want to come home with us once this was over. I was attached to him. It might have been Durga's influence though.

"OK, do the soldiers know what to do?" I asked.

"Kill fallen vampires?" Peri asked. When I nodded, she said, "That's pretty much all they do."

"Perfect," I said grabbing a cold chicken burger out of my greasy paper bag and taking a big bite. There was no way I was eating the cold McDonald's fires. I wished they had big macs here, but their cows are sacred and all that so the choices had been veggie burger or chicken and some of us need meat. "Give me ten minutes to fuel up, and we can go."

"I'll go tell the guys," Peri said, walking out of the room.

I took her place at the small table and set my greasy bag on the edge, so it didn't ruin the maps. Vincent stood by the door, his eyes glued to his phone.

"So, you good?" Frankie asked.

"Yup, I'm good," I said smiling. "How about you?" I asked raising my eyebrows.

He crinkled his nose. "This is awkward."

"It doesn't have to be. I like Peri."

The corner of his mouth ticked up at her name.

Frankie reached into my bag of fast food and grabbed a box of fries. He popped a couple in his mouth and then a few more. Gross. Cold french fries.

I ate another chicken burger and downed a bottle of juice, and I was ready.

"Let's get this show on the road," I called loud enough the vampires in the next room would hear me.

We all met in the parking lot and filed into vehicles.
Time to kill the demon.

CHAPTER ELEVEN

We pulled off the about an hour hike from the cave, cross-country. There was no way we could get any closer and still hide the vehicles. Luckily, I had recently done quite a bit of walking, and the vampires had endless energy. Most had a sword strapped to their backs although some had knives at their hips. Vincent looked like a soldier in his boots and army pants. The strap across his chest and handle of a long sword poked up over his shoulder making me want to eat him up. He was badass. I forced myself not to watch as he walked and muscles rippled under his tight t-shirt.

Singh swaggered along beside me, never out of reach. My will and determination. I took a deep breath. The night air had cooled, and the haunting call of some unseen bird cut through the night. The moon was full, offering enough light to see by, but also that unearthly feeling that poured tension into the atmosphere. I wanted to creep in, but I also wanted to race forward to end this faster.

The vampires walked on silent feet behind me. A few times I had to look over my shoulder to make sure they were still there.

In the car, we decided Frankie would zip ahead and make sure that there was no one in the area around the caves. I didn't want security or the police swarming us.

Frankie appeared before me, startling me out of my thoughts. He gave me a thumbs up and then he turned and walked beside me down into a gully. Up ahead was the Velganga river which flowed over the cliff and ran between us and the caves. I had seen it on the map. We would have to take the road to cross it, leaving us vulnerable if Mahishasura had a lookout. I was betting the buffalo didn't bother with a lookout though. He seemed confident in his own power and invincibility. We had to get in the cave opening so Frankie could see where I needed to go once we lured the fallen vampires out.

We crept up out of the underbrush and onto the road. Tension ran through me, making me swivel my head around trying to see every direction at once. My anxiety was high, and I felt like someone was watching me. Durga took over and sent out my senses. All the fallen were underground. I should have thought to do that. I needed to get my shit together and focus. I took a deep breath and pushed forward.

Peri stepped up beside Frankie and me. We crossed the open area in front of the caves and moved towards the narrow opening. The world was eerily silent and still as if it were waiting for just the right moment--the earth, holding its breath.

Peri slipped into the narrow opening, pulling Frankie through with her. He was tall but was thin enough he just barely fit. After a moment he tumbled back out followed by Peri.

He stood up and dusted himself off and then nodded.

Now or never.

I called my knife to my hand and quickly slit the skin on my arm before I had the chance to second guess it.

Blood bloomed on my skin and pooled a moment before sliding off the side my arm to fall in the dirt. I walked to the cave entrance and held my arm there, letting the light breeze carry the scent of my blood down to the horde of hidden vampires.

Singh rubbed his massive head across my stomach and purred before he moved into position opposite me in front of the cave. There he waited for his first victim to come through.

I closed my eyes and sent out my senses; the vampires stirred and moved beneath the earth. Their sense of smell was a billion times better than mine. Like sharks in the water, they moved towards the scent. When I was sure they were all coming, I pulled my senses back in and checked on the soldiers. Everyone formed a semi-circle watching the gap in the rock. Vincent's eyes were on me. I smiled at him, and he smiled back like I hoped he would.

Soon I could hear the approaching feet shuffling in the cave. Fallen vampires would soon be upon us. I gave Frankie a nod, and he took my hand, using his magic he took me to the top of the cliff. Then disappeared and reappeared with Peri. I looked down on the scene below and waited. Every muscle in my body was ready to fight, but this was not my fight. I had to wait.

I sent out my senses and watched in my radar as the vampires flooded out through the narrow gap and the battle began. I saw Mahishasura still tucked away deep in the caves. He probably knew I was here by now, but it would take me some time to find my way down to him.

Several minutes passed as I waited for the tunnels to clear. The fallen vampires moved fast, but they could only exit one at a time. I made sure none exited through any other means, assuring myself that the fallen wouldn't attack from behind while Peri and I made our way through to Mahishasura. About a dozen fallen vampire stayed in caves near Mahishasura. A reasonable amount I was sure Peri and I could handle.

I took one last look at Vincent's light before pulling my senses back in and opening my eyes. They flooded the entire area with fighting — vampire vs Vampire. Singh's white fur glowed in the moonlight, shaking a fallen vampire, his teeth wrapped around its neck. Vincent's sword swung effortlessly taking out fallen vampires as they reached him. Bodies were already piling up, but so far it only looked like fallen vampires.

I turned to Frankie and nodded; it was time to go.

He took my hand, and a moment later I was in the pitch-black cave. My knife flashed into my hand, and I took out the tiny pen light I had stored in my pocket. A second later, Frankie and Peri shifted in too, and we moved forward.

We hadn't checked out the cave system past this room, but I could feel Durga pressing me forward, so I trusted her to lead us in the right direction.

Beneath my feet was a sandy stone floor, worn bare in the center from hundreds of vampire feet. The passage beyond the small open room was comfortable enough for Peri and me, but Frankie had to stoop, so he didn't bump his head. The stone walls muffled the sounds of the raging battle and the further we walked the quieter it grew. When we came to a fork in the cave, Durga shoved me to the right, and we continued another hundred feet before it spilled out into a cavern. The intricately carved walls were like the rest of the caves in Ellora. The ceiling was delicate scrollwork that rolled down the walls to form people. Gods and Goddesses in various poses protruded from the stone. Some had flakes of paint on the surface, hinting at the beautiful colours this room would have had a thousand years ago.

Steps, carved into the stone, led down towards the center of the room where a smooth rock protruded from a tiny river. In the Hindu religion, people worshiped their Gods by pouring water or milk over a rock, called a lingam. When I walked in the desert, I watched people in the small villages doing this. They did this daily to praise Shiva, the creator of all things.

I stepped over the trickle of water and down another set of stone steps into a narrow passage. The tunnel continued to narrow until I had to turn sideways again and scraped against the stone walls. I looked back and realized that Frankie had gotten stuck. He couldn't go any further. I stopped and waited as he backed out until Peri could get ahead of him. Guess I wasn't taking my warlock with me. Peri caught up and gave me a thumbs up before patting her short sword. Crazy woman was almost as bloodthirsty as Durga. The Goddess, annoyed at the slowdown, gave me a shove and I scrapped my arm painfully against the rough stone wall.

Jerk Goddess.

I scooted along the ever-narrowing passage. Wishing I hadn't eaten those two chicken burgers at the motel and the third one in the car on the ride here. Elliot would have a squished head if it got any narrower, but the penlight disappeared into the darkness ahead giving me no sign of the length of the passage. Children must have carved it. Or maybe there was something to the aliens theory. It was slow going, but after what was probably only another hundred feet, the tunnel opened. Another fifty feet and I could walk straight again.

I took a breath to calm my nerves and closed my eye, sending out my senses. Hopefully, we were getting close. As soon as the dots of light appeared, I pulled my senses back in realizing a moment too late a fallen vampire was right in front of me. A body slammed into me, banging my head back onto the stone floor and teeth latched onto my arm as I raised it to protect my neck. The teeth bit down hard like a bulldog and broke the bone in my forearm. I screamed.

A moment later the body went limp, and Peri heaved it off me. Hopefully, it was Peri. I lost my penlight and couldn't see anything. Durga rose, her superior vision allowing me to see around me. It wasn't as good as my light, but I wouldn't be able to fight with a penlight either. Peri stood at my head, her blade, bloody in her hand. I hopped to my feet and gave her a pat on the shoulder.

Luckily the gross vampire had bit my left arm, and it was already healing, so I soldiered on. The tunnel took a left turn and then came to another fork. Durga pushed me one way, but I was sure I had seen vampires the other way with my senses. I didn't want them to come up behind us, but I had to get to Mahishasura.

"There are some down there." I pointed. "Buffalo this way," I whispered. Not that being quiet mattered anymore, but there was something about the tension that made me want to be quiet. Peri gave me a salute, then turned and marched towards the fallen vampires, leaving me alone to face my demon.

I took a few steps forward, wanting to send out my senses, but not wanting to close my eyes for even a moment after the last time. I focussed ahead and didn't notice someone creep up behind me until a hand fell on my shoulder.

CHAPTER TWELVE

I spun, calling my blade. In an instant, I had the foe pinned to the wall, my knife at his neck and nearly impaled in his spine before my eyes settled on the familiar face of Alex.

I pulled my knife back quickly, but a trickle of blood still ran from his neck.

"Thank you, goddess," he whispered as I considered stabbing him, anyway.

"What the fuck are you doing here?" I whispered yelled.

"I have to crown the king," he whispered back.

I threw my hands up and pushed him forward. I was not letting that weasel stay at my back. Just what I needed, someone to divert my attention from my real target. No time to argue. I gave him another shove, and we stepped into another larger room. The walls here were more like a mural. They showed a battle between animals and humans. It reminded me of Frankie's warehouse with the dragons on the ceiling except this was full of tigers and serpents.

As I scanned the room, I finally found my target. Mahishasura sat on a raised platform, his legs crossed and one hand raised as though he were a God.

I laughed at the absurdity. Or maybe it was Durga. She and I were so close now, I wasn't sure where I ended, and she began.

"You mock me now. You will not laugh when I am through with you."

The buffalo man launched himself off his platform, his teeth bared and small horns aimed for my chest. Durga became flesh as my arms multiplied and her trident raised a half second before the buffalo impacted. The force of him hitting the trident pushed me back across the stone, but I stayed on my feet. Mahishasura landed against the far wall, his momentum carrying him. Dust rained down from the ceiling, and I had a passing worry about a cave in but pushed it away to focus on the biggest threat. Mahishasura transformed into his full buffalo form. His horns scraped the ceiling as he lifted his head and bellowed a hollow sound. His head was as tall as my whole body. When his eyes locked on me, a puff of foul air blew from his nose. I knew it was now or never.

Durga pulled forth her long sword. I swung it once before the beast charged. His ragged hair shuddered as he lurched forward. One more long stride and he was bearing down on me. I leaped forward for momentum and slid to the ground between his thick hooved legs. I stabbed upwards into his stomach. Blood gushed from the wound as he passed above me. He let out an angry roar. I leapt and spun as he turned to face me again.

I jumped to my feet, and Durga switched to her conch shell. She brought it to my lips and blew into the end. The sound was like a low whistle that rang through the temple and caused the buffalo to yell in pain. He dropped to his knees for a moment before shaking his massive head, his ragged fur waving and getting back to his feet.

He charged again, this time there was no warning. Durga attempted to draw back on her bow to launch an arrow, but he was too close, and his horn reached us before we could move. The long sharp horn impaled through my sternum and out through my back before slamming me into the wall of the cave, pinning me like a bug. I screamed looking down at the horn that blasted through my body so close to baby Elliot that a new wave of anger hit me.

I slammed the arrow still in my hand down into Mahishasura's head; it stuck under his skin, and he roared again, but it didn't do any real damage.

Durga waved her arms until her club came forward. We swung it down onto the buffalo's head as hard as possible, and the sound it created was like a struck gong. The buffalo collapsed to the ground, his horn dropping to the side and forcing me to slide off. The pain was overwhelming, but I had no time to focus on that. Durga pushed it away and forced me to my feet though blood sprayed from my chest and back like a waterfall. My arms and legs stayed true, and Durga brought forth the lotus.

Its delicate petals seemed a strange weapon to use on a raging buffalo, but peace fell over me like a blanket. That was when I saw the white lion swagger through the doorway. My vision was growing weak, fluttery like a delicate bird.

Singh stepped up to the Buffalo who began to rise, his thick legs scrambling on the stone floor made slick by my blood. Singh let out a thunderous roar. His teeth glistened in his mouth. He set one paw on the great buffalo's nose, pinning him to the floor. His other massive paw reared back and came down so fast, it wasn't clear what he had done until the head of the buffalo fell away from the body. He had sliced the demon's head clean off with his razor-sharp talons. Blood sprayed for a moment from the decapitated head and then oozed to cover the entire floor of the temple.

My vision was wavering when a figure approached me. It wasn't until Alex's face came into view a few inches from my own that I realized it was him.

"Please, I must crown the king. Now is the time." Alex held out his hand.

I didn't know what he wanted. I shook my head.

"Please, Goddess! The time is now! The King of Thunder waits!" Alex's voice rose to nearly a scream as my knees buckled and I collapsed to the floor.

"Goddess!" He yelled, his voice was fading. The sound of Singh's purr pulled me back from the gloom, and Alex's words reached my mind.

The woman at the rest stop said I had to give the King of Thunder back his lightning. I didn't know what that meant, but I had a lightning bolt. Durga produced it, holding it in front of me to inspect. I looked from the gift to Alex. Did I trust him with something so powerful? I didn't trust him with anything.

I knew I only had moments to decide; I struggled to look Alex in the eye. I couldn't speak. My throat was full of blood. My body convulsed trying to get me to cough, but it would do no good. There was a hole through my rib cage. I held out the lightning bolt with the last of my strength, praying it was the right thing to do.

I watched Alex's back disappear out the door and turned my face into Singh's thick fur. I prayed I would pass out, as Durga receded, the pain washed in. More pain than I knew a body could handle. Somehow, I stayed conscious for several moments, but my heart beat slowed with every second.

The floor shook, and I thought maybe the cave would collapse after all. It shook again and again as I prayed for death. Durga had abandoned me. I felt her presence like a phantom limb. The space she occupied was now vacant, and I was hollow. A tear slipped down my cheek to get lost in the fur of my lion. My will. He protected me in life and now in death. I imagined I could see my heart, taking one last shuttering beat, before it stopped. The silence was complete.

A harsh tongue ran across my face as I faded away.

"No!" A voice shook the room with its force. "You will not leave me!"

The sound pulled me back from the darkness, and my heart gave a single squeeze. I thought of Elliot. His beautiful face and small fingers. His blond hair and blue eyes.

My heart gave another valiant squeeze.

"Come back!" The voice was so loud, like thunder ringing in my ears and shaking my body.

My eyes flicked open on the third squeeze of my empty heart, and a man was before me -- not a man, a God. He sat astride a white elephant. His four arms each bore a weapon, one of which was Durga's lightning bolt.

The elephant raised its trunk and thundered a sound, a flash of light so bright, it blew out my vision, and I couldn't see for a moment. When I could see again, the man stood over me.

"You cannot die," the man said, his voice stern. His hair whipped in the wind that blew through the cavern.

"I will do as I please," my voice said. I only realized after I had spoken that I could speak. I lifted a hand and pressed it to my chest. It was whole again. Durga had left me, but I had healed anyway.

I looked back to the man. His eyes faded to a soft blue and suddenly Vincent was standing over me. He fell to his knees and slid his arms under me, lifting me from the floor and cradling me in his arms. His forehead fell to mine, and then his lips met mine too and heat rushed through me. I relaxed my muscles uncoiling and conforming to his body. He rose and carried me from the room where the dead Buffalo lay. He walked through halls that were now wide and tall enough to walk through on an elephant.

"Did you do this?" I asked him.

"I suppose so, though I'm not clear on what I can do and what Indra does. I would have dug it by hand to get to you."

I put my hand to my stomach and held my breath. "I don't feel him."

"He is there. I can hear his heart. It's strong," Vincent said, and I let out a sigh. When we exited the tunnel into the moonlight, the carnage covered the area. Soldiers were checking bodies and decapitating fallen vampires who weren't thoroughly dead.

I glanced around the area. "Where is Peri," I said.

"Right here," she said as she came trotting up beside us. "You look like shit."

"Thanks, you don't look so hot yourself. What happened to your hair?" I asked. She had a giant bald spot.

"Some fallen bastard thought he could use it as a handle. I reminded him that today's women don't like grabby men and cut off his hands before I cut off his head." She rubbed her bare scalp. "I hope it grows back quickly. It messes up my style."

I laughed, cringing at the ache that still ran through my chest.

A line of vans came rolling up, and Vincent shuffled me into one. I lay on the backseat and waited for the rest of the soldiers and crew to finish whatever they were doing. I kept one hand on my stomach and waited, rejoicing in the occasional tiny flutters there. It was so reassuring and consuming I didn't notice a body block the van doorway.

"I'm leaving, Lark."

My eyes darted to the van door to find Singh in human form, his face lined in sadness.

"You don't have to go," I said.

He bit his lip and looked away. "I can't go back to the city. You don't need my help now. You have your own magic and now that Mahishasura is dead and Durga has left..."

"So, she's really gone?" I cut in.

"Yes. She left behind soldiers to continue her work, including you. She will return someday when she needs to restore the balance again."

I bit my lip and nodded holding back the tears. Everything was changing so fast. Durga hadn't even said goodbye. "Thank you, Singh, for all you have done for me. I will miss you."

"You can come visit me. I'll be here," he said before shifting back into a lion and letting out an ear-shattering roar. He turned and ran. I struggled to sit up then watched him climb the rocky cliff to stand above the Ellora caves. His yellow eyes glowed in the moonlight, and his white coat glistened. Then he disappeared beyond the cliff.

I pulled my knees up to my chest and wrapped my arms around them, hugging them tightly.

When Vincent returned, he reached in and scooped me out of the van. He kissed the top of my head as he set me in the passenger seat of the car Peri and I drove across the country. He slid into the driver's seat, and I heard the two back doors open and close.

Vincent started the car without a word and drove us back to the motel. When he pulled up, there was no line of vehicles behind us. I turned around and realized it was Frankie and Peri in the back seat.

"Everyone else is heading home," Vincent said. "Alex said to say goodbye. He's going back to Moscow."

That was for the best. I would probably hold a grudge against him forever. Though I guess he came through in the end.

"We will stay here for tonight and leave in the morning," Vincent said before he stepped out of the car. He came around and opened my door. I started to get up, but pain ricocheted through my chest, and Vincent scooped me up. I didn't like to him carrying me. It made me feel weak, like a kitten.

"You'll feel better tomorrow," Vincent whispered as he unlocked the door to the motel room.

"Someone should check on Ninel. Let him know I am not Durga in case he wants to go back to Moscow," I said, my voice a little more bitter than I intended.

"I'll do that now," he said as he set me down on the bed.

As soon as the motel room door shut behind him, I rolled off the bed and limped to the bathroom. I left the door open in case I fell down and killed myself, but turned on the shower and tried to peel my clothes off. The blood was sticky, and the fabric clung to my skin. That car would look like we slaughtered someone in it tomorrow. I kicked off my shoes and toed off my socks. My pants were heavy with blood, so they fell easily, but I struggled with my shirt for several minutes before Vincent returned and found me.

I dropped my arms and let the tears fall. I wasn't even sure why I was crying.

"I'm all alone," I whispered before a sob wracked my broken, fragile human body. Even before I knew about Durga, she had been there. This hollow feeling was new and uncomfortable. Vincent stepped forward and wrapped his arms around me, burying my head in his chest.

"Never," he whispered, making the sobs come faster and fiercer. Vincent held me tight until I calmed. Mourning the loss of my inner goddess was weird considering what she put me through. "I will always be with you," Vincent said, taking away the sting of loneliness.

Little birds flapped in my stomach, reminding me that I wasn't alone, even in my skin. Elliot was growing inside me, and soon I would have the family I always wished for.

Elliot would have the greatest family ever even if it didn't include Singh. The lion's absence was as obvious as the lack of soft snores coming from the bed.

He would have uncles and a whole coven of people to care about him. He would have a nice kitchen lady to make him snacks and Uncle Frankie to teach him about magic. I took a deep breath and steeled myself. I pushed away from Vincent's chest and looked up into his blue eyes. Maybe Durga wasn't with me anymore, but Vincent still looked like a vampire. His pointed teeth peek through his lips. If I was just a human, I shouldn't be able to see his teeth. I tucked that information away for another day and pulled at the neck of my shirt. "Help me."

He tore the thin material and gently pulled my arms free. I stepped into the steaming shower, and Vincent stepped in with me.

"You still have your clothes on," I said.

"I don't need to be naked to wash your hair, Lark." He grabbed the bottle of shampoo and stood there all wet and glorious while I ducked under the running water. He turned me around and squirted shampoo on my head. His fingers massaged my scalp, relieving some of my tension. I held my hand over my stomach, assuring myself that Elliot was fine. My little miracle. My chest bore a huge scar. None of my previous injuries had left a mark, but this one had, and I wondered if it was because Durga had left me there to die. If so, how had I healed? These were questions for another day. My body was already protesting being upright for so long. My vision shimmered around the edges. I leaned back into Vincent's chest and let the water wash away the rest of the dried and flaky blood.

Once I was clean, Vincent wrapped me in a big towel and dried my hair while I sat on the bed. Sitting was better than standing, but still hurt. He pulled one of his big sweaters over my head before tucking me in and kissing my forehead. Then he went back to the bathroom, and I heard water hitting him as he had his shower. I listened to the domestic sound and let my eyes slip shut.

CHAPTER THIRTEEN

The scent of bacon and coffee raised me from the dead. Ok, I wasn't dead, but something might have died in my mouth. It was a new day, and I tried to put the pain of the previous day behind me. Until I sat up. Then I remembered I don't have super healing powers anymore, and I collapsed to the bed again.

"Morning Lark," my bestie said.

I raised a hand and waved.

"You still lying around? Get up lazy. We have a plane to catch." Peri said.

I flipped her off.

"If you don't get up, I'm eating all this bacon and drinking all this coffee," she said.

I heard the door to the room open and close.

"Stop tormenting her or I will cut off your head," Vincent's stern voice said.

I sat up and glared at him. "Hey. You don't get to threaten my friend," I said, pointing a finger at him.

"That is how you get Lark out of bed," Vincent said with a grin.

Peri laughed, but I continued to scowl at the vampire lord.

He stepped forward and stole a kiss before setting a plastic bag down on the bed beside me. "I got you some clothes. Comfortable for travelling. It's a long flight."

I grabbed onto his shoulders and tried to pull myself off the mattress, but I was stuck in the blankets that had wrapped around me somehow overnight. A lion used to hold the sheets down on one side. The thought made me miss Singh again, but I wouldn't cry. Damn it.

Vincent untangled the blankets and then lifted and set me on my feet. I had to hunch over because my chest still hurt. A flutter made me set my hand on my stomach. There was a small bump where none had been the day before. I froze and waited. The bird flapped its wings, much stronger than the day before. Little kicks and twirls felt more like a fish than a bird.

Vincent noticed me holding my stomach, and his hand slid to join mine.

"Oh my god," he whispered. "You should change and eat. We should get home." His voice was a little worried, but I knew everything was fine. Elliot was twisting and leaping, how could anything be wrong? I would need to get him into sports, or maybe martial arts. That would serve him well. Not that he would need to fight. I would protect him.

I shook out of my visions of Elliot's future and grabbed the bag of clothes before heading to the bathroom.

"Guard my bacon," I said over my shoulder.

I came back out dressed in jogging pants and a hoodie that was loose and comfortable, just as Vincent had promised. I grabbed the small tray of bacon and a cup of coffee off the table then walked out the door. When we loaded back into the car, someone had covered my seat with a blanket. I bet those blood stains would never come out. I took a sip of the coffee, but it didn't taste right.

"It's decaf, you're pregnant," Peri said with a laugh when she saw my face.

Gross.

I put it in the cup holder and left it there.

Ninel was with us, his cheeks were flush, though he was still thin. He looked like a sick man now though, instead of a skeleton. He was bouncing back faster than Trevor had.

"Hey, Ninel. You headed back to Moscow?" I asked. Frankie and Peri slipped into the seats on either side of the ancient vampire.

"No, I am coming back to America with you. I will guard the child if you allow me." He bowed his head.

"Of course. I would be honoured. But you know Durga left?" I asked, to be sure.

"Yes, Vincent informed me, but she is never gone, Lark. She would approve of my mission to see you and your child safe."

The hairs rose on the back of my neck. He was right. The goddess was always watching, just not through my eyes anymore.

"Thank you, Ninel," I whispered.

Vincent started the car and drove us to the airport. He pulled up to the doors and let me out. I waited with Frankie for the vampires to park.

"I'm glad you came," I said to fill the awkward silence.

"I'm glad I came too. I wasn't sure how it would feel to be around you and Vincent, but it's ok. I feel like maybe we should have never been more than friends — good friends."

"I feel that way too," I said, smiling at him. "So. You and Peri?"

Frankie flung his arm over my shoulders and pulled me in tight beside him. "I don't want to jinx anything, but she is amazing. Isn't she?" We watched as the vampires walked across the parking lot. I tried to get my eyes to shift from Vincent, but it was like he had hypnotized me. He was back in a suit and looked delicious. He had styled hair perfectly and wore dark sunglasses. Nope, it was too much. He was too beautiful.

"You drooling, Lark?" Frankie teased.

"You would be too, he's drool-worthy," I muttered, still distracted.

"I'll take your word for it," Frankie said.

Vincent took my hand and kissed my knuckles with a steamy grin on his face. Then he looped his arm around my shoulders, and we walked through the airport. It was just as busy today as last time we were here. We wandered around laughing as we tried to find the right gate when out of the crowd an old lady appeared in front of me.

Frankie gasped, but I couldn't take my eyes off the old woman. She had to be over one hundred. The lines on her face were deep valleys. She hunched over a cane and leaning heavily on it as if it were the only thing still keeping her upright.

"Finally," She whispered and reached out her hand towards my stomach. I lifted my hand to stop her, but

Frankie grabbed my arm, and the old woman's fingers pressed into the small bulge below my navel.

"Jayanta," she said before she backed a step and disappeared into the heavy flow of travellers.

I stood stunned for a minute and then turned on Frankie. "What the hell was that?"

"That was an ancient. She was older than the elders. Older than any I have ever met before."

"An ancient what?" I asked, still not putting the pieces together.

"Witch," he replied.

"That was her? Do you think it was the one who told Alex and that woman where to be?"

Frankie's face was pensive, but he didn't answer me.

"What does Jayanta mean?" I asked, not expecting an answer, but Peri piped up.

"He was the son of Indra."

The crowds moved around us like we were a rock in a river. I caught Vincent's eye his lip ticked up in an unusual way. It was Indra in charge. I wasn't sure how I knew, but he was there, looking out through Vincent's eyes.

"His name is Elliot," I said to the thunder God.

He bowed his head and slipped away, leaving Vincent in control again. Vincent ushered me to a gate. We all boarded in silence and took our seats in first class.

I was lost in thought through taxiing and takeoff. When they shut off the fasten seat belts light, I got up to go to the bathroom.

Vincent had a worried look on his face, but I flashed him a smile. It was fine, see. I smiled.

In the tiny airplane bathroom, I stared at myself in the mirror; it was strange to look at myself and not feel Durga looking back, but then it was strange to look at Vincent and see some other guy staring back. I guess what goes around, comes around. He lived with me and Durga; I can live with him and Indra.

I told myself I was just unsteady because of all the sudden changes. Once we were home and had space to relax, I would feel better.

Someone knocked at the door. "Just a sec." I splashed cold water on my face and fumbled with the lock. The door opened, and I saw Peri's face for a second before her hand shoved me back into the bathroom, and she slid the door shut behind us.

"What the..."

"Shh," she said, holding her finger to her lips. "I wanted to see if you were ok. The thing with the witch was weird, and I saw Vincent change and then change back. It was weird, right?"

I sighed. "Yeah, that was weird, but I used to do the same thing as Durga, so I can't complain."

Peri bit her lip. There wasn't much space between us up in the tiny bathroom. "I guess you are right, but you can still have a feeling about it. No one would blame you."

"Vincent might."

"Fuck him. Don't forget who you are just because you are all pregnant and in a relationship."

I snorted a laugh. "You're right." I took a deep breath. "I'll talk to him, but it's not like he can change it. Gods do what they want." Nobody knew that as well as I did.

"Still. He should know how you feel." Peri cracked her knuckles. "If you want me to fight him, I will."

"Oh my god, you are so weird."

"Yeah," she smiled.

I hugged her and pushed her back out of the tiny bathroom.

"Everything ok?" Vincent asked as I fell into the seat beside him.

"Yeah, just girl talk." In the middle of the Atlantic Ocean was not the place to discuss Gods and their offspring.

I set my seat back and put on the headphones to watch the movie. I must have dozed off because before I knew it, Vincent was shaking me awake.

"You should eat something," he said, and I realized there was a flight attendant with a food cart beside me.

"Oh, um, I guess a sandwich."

The woman smiled at me, and a snippet of a dream came back to me. I couldn't quite remember it, but it was at the edge of my mind as I ate. There was only a dark feeling. I stopped eating and looked out the window, trying to force my brain to chase the memory.

"What's wrong?" Vincent asked.

"I don't know. Just a weird dream," I said.

Vincent's eyes studied me for a minute. Then he went back to the laptop that was sitting on a small fold-down desk in front of him.

"What are you doing?" I asked.

"I'm putting your name on all my businesses and investments and updating my will. My lawyer sent me the paperwork while we were in India, so I'm just getting it all filled out so it will be official shortly after we land."

"Whoa. Why are you doing that?" I asked, staring at the screen filled with appendix C's and side notations.

"Because I want to make sure you are taken care of if anything were to happen to me. You and our son." He smiled and slid a hand over my stomach. The little nugget inside did a flip and karate kick making me giggle.

He smiled and watched my tiny belly jiggle.

A woman stopped in the aisle with a big smile on her face. "When are you due?" she asked.

My mouth hung open as I grappled for words. That was a typical question, right? People asked pregnant women that all the time but I had no idea. I mean, my belly was much bigger than it should be, considering I wasn't even a week pregnant. Luckily Vincent was quicker than me.

"Three more months," he said, and the woman moved along.

"Oh, my god. Shouldn't I be taking vitamins and seeing a doctor and eating a salad? I had bacon for breakfast! That's probably not healthy. I'm already failing at this." I covered my face with my hands.

"Stop freaking out," Vincent whispered. I could hear to humour in his voice.

"This is serious, Vincent. Why is everything so funny to you now?"

He leaned in close his eyes on mine. "I almost died. Almost lost everything. And now I've got everything I ever wanted. I got the girl and the family." He reached into his pocket and pulled out a little box, and my heart pounded so loud I could hear it in my ears.

"I am the luckiest man to walk the earth," he said as he opened the box and pulled out a diamond ring. "And the only way I would be happier is if you said yes and agreed to spend eternity with me." He slipped the ring on my finger. It sparkled in the sun coming through the tiny airplane window.

"That is a huge rock," Peri's voice cut in. I glanced over at her, and she and Frankie were watching on, both smiling.

I looked back to Vincent still stunned.

"Say yes," he said with a laugh.

"Yes," I said. He swooped in and kissed me as the rest of the first-class passengers cheered and clapped. I hadn't even realized they were watching us.

When he pulled away, he was still smiling. He looked so much like his twin with the happiness on his face.

"Shotgun wedding!" Peri cried over the crowd.

I shot her a look. "Why am I friends with you?" I called back.

She used her fingers and thumbs to form the shape of a heart and mouthed the words "I love you. I shook my head.

Holy shit, I was getting married.

CHAPTER FOURTEEN

When the plane landed, there was a limo waiting for us at the airport and Drew stood by the door.

"Hey, listen, I'm sorry for how things went down, Drew," I said as I stopped in front of him. His eyes flashed to my stomach and then back to my face.

"It's cool. You know, I didn't take it personally," he said, but he didn't sound believable.

"I'm still sorry for kicking you out and leaving you in Russia."

He nodded. I would make it up to him.

We climbed int he limo, Vincent, and I sat together and Peri and Frankie and then there was Ninel. He was looking rough again. His eyes kept rolling closed, but Drew sat beside him and hooked him up to an IV in the back seat of the moving vehicle. I had no idea that Drew could do that.

The car rolled through the city and past my old store and old apartment building. Frankie pointed out his warehouse to Peri.

"I need a liaison for the magic community," Vincent said. "Peri, if you are up for it, I would like you to fill that role."

She looked from Vincent to Frankie and back again. "Sure, sounds like fun."

"Perfect, I will have your employment papers written up," Vincent said, sounding more like the boss he was as we closed in on his mansion. I knew the relaxed Vincent wouldn't last. The vampires of the city wouldn't take him seriously if he were a happy-go-lucky guy. Without Durga, it would take work to keep the city safe. I rubbed my stomach.

The steel gates slid open at the end of the driveway, and the limo glided up the tree-lined lane. It pulled to a stop at the door, and a second later a small vampire flung the car door open and had his arms wrapped around my neck.

"Hey Trevor," I said with a laugh.

"I was so worried. They sent me home from Jaisalmer, but I wanted to stay and help. I could have fought. I'm getting strong, you know," he took a breath, and in that brief pause, he glanced down, noticing my stomach. His eyes shot up, a look of shock etched into his face. He looked back down and tentatively rested a hand on my stomach. Elliot did his patented karate kick, and Trevor jumped back, bumping his head on the roof of the car. Everyone else had already snuck out around him.

"You have a baby?" he whispered, more a statement than a question. I remembered him playing with all the babies at the mom and tot yoga classes. He was a natural with babies.

"Elliot. I'll need your help. I have no idea what to do with a baby."

Trevor looked up again, his eyes rimmed with tears. "Can I be Uncle Trevor?"

"He'll be so lucky to have you as his uncle."

Trevor wrapped his arms around my waist and hugged my stomach. When he pulled away, he helped me out of the car. Everyone else had gone into the mansion already. Trevor and I climbed the steps, his hand on my elbow like I was a delicate old lady. I guess I was more fragile than before. We walked through the door and into the tall foyer. I remembered the first time I had walked in. My fear seemed so ridiculous, looking back.

"I'm going to order you some books on babies, Lark. You will be the best mom," Trevor said as he hustled off down the hall, leaving me standing alone in the beautiful entrance.

My cheeks pulled up into a smile, and I felt calmer about having a baby, knowing I had help.

I started up the stairs to head for my old room, hoping it was still there when a voice behind me stopped me.

"You did it." Vlad's accent echoed through the foyer.

I turned on the stairs, and he was standing there, looking every bit the old-fashioned vampire. Vlad and I worried together for months before I finally ran off to find Vincent.

"It's been quiet here. Thank you for bringing him home."

I nodded and climbed the stairs. I walked to my old room, but when I swung the door open, it was empty. Not a trace of me remained there.

"Your stuff is in our room," Vincent said from behind me.

Startled, I spun around and bumped into his chest, my hands wrapped around him and I relaxed in his arms for a moment. His hands rubbed up and down my back.

"We need a baby room," I said. "Elliot needs his own room."

He smiled down at me. "Ok, I'll call a contractor to put a door in from our room to the one next to it."

I nodded, and he put his arm around me, leading me to his room. It was just as I remembered it — the tall bed and antique furniture. Nothing had changed, except that all my clothes were hanging in his closet, too.

"I think I'll have a bath and a nap. I didn't sleep well on the plane," I said.

"All right. Our lawyer will be here soon. I have a bit of work to do, but I will wake you up for dinner."

I ran a hot bath with tons of bubbles and felt my aching muscles relax. I missed Durga for her healing ability if nothing else. I was sure I wouldn't be fighting rogue vampires if this was how long it would take for me to heal from an injury.

When the hot water had sufficiently pruned me, I stepped out of the deep tub and got dressed in some of my old yoga pants and a tank top. I curled up under the blankets and was asleep within minutes.

—

Men and women swarmed around me. They were small like elves or leprechauns. That thought brought forward a man dressed in green velvet. His tiny suit and dapper hat made him look exactly like a leprechaun, but I knew he wasn't. I had met him once before when Vincent had brought me to an old logging road, and we walked until a small house appeared. Inside had been a giant warehouse of short men and women forging steel blades. That was where I had chosen my blade. The one Durga and I used to fight fallen vampires. My magic knife.

"We have been waiting for our king. Bring him to us." The man in green said. "We have a gift he must receive so he will grow to know who he is."

—

I screamed and bolted awake, sitting up in bed so fast, the room spun. My breaths were heaving, and a cold sweat had packed my hair to my forehead. I raised my hand to wipe my brow, but my knife was in it. I thought the blade only worked because of Durga, but here it was.

The door flung open, banging against the wall and Vincent stood before me with a look of murder in his eyes.

"It was a dream," I panted.

Vincent noticed the blade in my hand and his face morphed from violent to concerned.

"What kind of dream?" he took a few steps closer to the end of the bed but looked cautious. I set the knife on the bedside table.

"I don't know. I saw the elf, the one who gave me this blade."

"Emanuel?"

"Yeah. He said to bring them their king, and that they had gifts. For some reason, the dream scared me. He wasn't threatening. Was he talking about you?"

"I don't think so. I have nothing to do with the elves, neither does Indra."

I rubbed my stomach. That was why it scared me. They wanted to see Elliot, but how he could be their king was beyond me. He was me and Vincent's child. Or maybe Indra's, but that had nothing to do with the elves. I bit my lip and stared at Vincent who seemed lost in confusion too.

"It was just a dream," I said. "My mind is weird."

Vincent didn't look convinced. "I'll go talk to Emanuel." He stepped forward and kissed my forehead, then retreated and shut the door behind him as he left.

I fell back down into the pillows. Being me was too weird.

A few minutes later I heard my door open, and as I was about to sit up, Peri flew over me to land on the bed beside me. A giant grin on her face.

"All you do is laze about. Let's go do yoga and get food," she said. She sounded off. Like she was parroting back something or following orders.

"Did he tell you to keep an eye on me?" I asked, meaning Vincent, and we both knew it.

"Yes, but he doesn't realize that I am a terrible influence on you yet. Once you are no longer pregnant and back in fighting form, it will be too late, and we will be up to all kinds of no good."

I laughed until tears rolled down my cheeks. Oh, man, Vincent had no idea what he was in for.

"Come on, lazy butt. You gotta be in tip-top shape to chase this baby around."

She hopped up, and I rolled out of bed to follow her.

We passed a few vampires in the halls who gave me a nod. Some of them I recognized, but there were some new faces too. I should probably get to know them since I was settling down here. The thought of settling down made me itchy. We would see how long that lasted. Peri took the steps to the main floor two at a time. I was more careful since I wasn't as indestructible as before.

The gym was the same as it was — a large clear area on one side used for sparring and weights and exercise machines on the other. The smell of sweat and blood lingered on the air and pulled up a bit of adrenaline. It was weird not having Durga pushing at me. It made me feel kind of sluggish.

Peri sat down, crossing her legs and I joined her, sitting far enough away we both had space.

I took deep calming breaths, and Elliot seemed to slow too. He still wiggled, but it was less karate and more yoga speed. I moved into the opening movements, catching Peri out of the corner of my eye as she mirrored me. The stretches started painfully. Deep pulls and sharp stabs soon gave way, softening until I felt pliant. My body remembered the way it was designed to work. The popping and snapping sounds coming from my joints and spine were proof it had forgotten. I balanced on one foot, imagining roots sinking deep into the floor and wished I was outside. I imagined the sky above me and the sun kissing my cheeks. I pictured grass beneath me as I swept my fingers down to stretch out my lumbar. I crawled my fingers forward across my imaginary lawn. I felt the soft breeze on my skin as it rippled through the tree leaves and then I stretched up to touch the sky again.

Yelling startled me out of my happy place, and when I opened my eyes, I was standing outside Vincent's house, on his back lawn.

I looked around, trying to figure out what had just happened. I was sure I was in the gym when I closed my eyes. I spun around as the yelling got louder, and Ninel raced out the back door.

"Lark! Holy crap," he said. He bent at the waist and rested his hands on his knees, his breath heaving in and out.

"What happened? Why are you running? You should be resting," I said.

"Yes, well, when vampires began racing around calling your name and searching the house, I got concerned and thought maybe I should help look." Several other vampires came pushing out the door followed closely behind by Peri.

"What the hell, you crazy woman!" Peri yelled.

"I have no idea," I said in reply.

Peri whipped out her phone and sent a text. She popped it back in her pocket, and then Frankie was in the yard.

"What the hell?" he said, looking at me.

"I don't know. I was in the basement. Then I was here."

"Is she a witch?" Peri asked.

"No, I would know if she was." He squinted at me, and his eyes went far away like he was looking through me then snapped back. "I don't know what she is."

"I am not a what," I said. "I'm a who." I stomped past all the staring eyes and jogged up to my room, slamming the door behind me.

Something was weird, but I didn't need everyone studying me like an insect. I climbed back into bed and pulled the blanket over my head. The sunlight streaming in the window trickled through the blanket, but it was dark enough and warm.

I lay curled up I there until a voice spoke from outside my fort.

"Lark." It was Frankie.

"Go away," I said.

"I want to talk to you," he said.

"No, thank you," I replied. Closing my eyes to try and block out the world.

The blankets on the other side of the bed popped up for a second, blinding me with daylight until Frankie slid in and pulled the covers down again.

"You shouldn't be in here," I said, rolling onto my side to face him.

"I'm just worried about you."

"Well, I'm used to weird things happening now, so it's not worth worrying about." It was a lie. I was not cool with this new development. The elves and the magical transportation thing was not normal.

Frankie nodded. "You remember I can read your mind, right?"

"Shit," I muttered, and he chuckled. "Elves have weird powers."

"I'm not an elf. I'm just short," I said, pulling my knees towards my chest, I cradled my small round stomach in my lap.

"Ok, you want to go get a sandwich?"

"I could go for a Big Mac," I replied.

He laughed and took my hand. Suddenly we were in the driveway standing in front of Frankie's shiny motorcycle.

"Did you bring this with you?" I asked, sure he had shifted himself into the yard after Peri texted him.

"I'd just got on when Peri sent a text to say you were missing. It's the heaviest thing I've ever moved," he said with a cocky grin. He pulled a helmet out and handed it to me. I pulled it on and fiddled with the snap until he reached over and snapped it for me.

Frankie swung his leg over the bike and held it upright while I scampered. I hooked my sock feet up on the tiny bars and wrapped my arms around his waist. The bike screamed to life, and Frankie drove us out the driveway, stopping at the gate. The vampire at the gate looked at us for a minute. I gave him a wave to hurry him up. I wanted to hit the road.

The guard picked up a phone and made a call. Frankie flicked off the engine and crossed his arms over his chest, waiting.

I watched the guard's lips move, but I couldn't hear him even when I strained my ears. I no longer had Durga's help with the super vamp hearing.

After a moment he walked out and handed me the phone. I shook my head and took the phone.

"What?" I said, in my least happy voice.

"Where are you going?"

Ah, there is the grumpy bossy vampire I knew. Guess the honeymoon is over.

"I'm going out. Is there a problem?"

"On a motorcycle? That's dangerous."

Frankie scoffed. He could hear the vampire on the line.

"Tough shit, Vincent. You tell this vampire to open the gates right now," I said. I didn't have much of a threat to offer. I wasn't nearly as scary as Durga.

There was a long pause. I waited.

"Open the gates," he said before the line went dead. Shit head.

I dropped the phone on the asphalt and wrapped my arms around Frankie. The guard who had been listening in to the conversation ran back to the booth and hit the button to open the gates.

As soon as they slid open, Frankie sped through and then off down the road. He didn't break any laws, but he took corners at speed and accelerated faster than necessary. Adrenaline hit my system making me giddy. I clung to Frankie until he pulled into a McDonald's.

"You want to eat here or take it to go?" Frankie asked.

"To go. I want to get out of the city."

He smiled and slipped into the drive-through. Once we had a bag of food, Frankie had me hop off and grab a backpack out of his motorcycle bag. I put the food in it, hoping it would stay warm and then jumped back on and we took off down the highway. The wind whipped my face, and I tucked in behind Frankie to use him as a wind block. It wasn't long before he got off the highway and took me to a quiet place I recognized. We had picnicked here before. I hopped off, and Frankie kicked out the kickstand. He grabbed a blanket from his bag, and we walked down a narrow path to the grassy hillside.

Laying on the blanket in the sun and stuffing my face with big macs was like heaven. The difference between here and India, besides the obvious, was that in India it was a dry heat, here there was humidity that made it feel different. More like spring.

"I shouldn't have brought you here," Frankie said.

"Why not?" I tipped my head to look at him.

Frankie sighed. "You two are just working out stuff, and this thing with Peri is brand new. I don't want to cause problems."

"Well, I wanted a burger, and Mr. Bossy-pants isn't the boss of me. He needs a reminder. Everything is weird, but you and I are friends, and I have hardly seen you in months. Also, Peri and I are bff's so she won't mind that I'm out here with you."

Frankie raised his hands in defeat. "Ok, but if it becomes a big deal, I'll back off. I just don't like to see you hiding in a blanket fort."

I laughed, and Frankie lay back. We watched the clouds move across the sky.

"Is your coven still afraid of me?" I asked, my eyes tracking a cloud that looked like a lion.

"No, I think you are fine now. Anytime you want to visit, you can."

"That's good. I've missed being around you. I like that we can be here and it's not awkward. That's what I always liked about you, Frankie. Except when we argued, it was always easy."

He smiled at me, and we lay there for almost an hour in silence watching the clouds before we packed up the garbage and headed back to the mansion.

Time to have a chat with my monster fiancé.

CHAPTER FIFTEEN

Frankie flew back through town, making me smile so wide, my face muscles were a bit sore when he slowed and steered the bike through the gates to Vincent's mansion. He pulled up to the steps at the front of the house and let me off, then he smiled at me and rode back down the driveway. I watched him go and then turned to track down Vincent. Hopefully, he was home from visiting the elves and would have information, but first, he and I needed to talk. I was dreading it, but I wouldn't walk on eggshells. He had no right to tell me what to do.

I climbed the steps, and the door swung open, revealing Trevor.

"Hey Lark, I'm just showing Andre the ropes."

Andre was a human. He was no more than twenty. His hair swept up into a high man-bun and his clothes made him look like he belonged in a cafe working on his novel.

He had his sleeves rolled up, displaying tattoos. He wore a fashionable scarf around his neck and his rough beard completed the picture of a modern man.

"Andre. It's good to meet you."

"You too. I've read the file on you, and Trevor explained you are pregnant. Congratulations, I look forward to meeting your little one, and if there is anything you need, please let me know." Andre didn't sound like I expected. He sounded professional, smiled and seemed honestly polite.

Trevor beamed at the man like he was brilliant. Interesting.

"Thanks, Andre." I turned to Trevor. "Is Vincent home yet?"

"Not yet. He called to say he's on his way. He wanted to talk to you, but I told him you were still out. I hope that's OK."

"Yeah, that's fine. Thanks."

I took the first hall and bypassed the dining room in favour of the kitchen. I walked in and almost died. It smelled like chocolate cake. My favourite kitchen lady was icing it at the counter, but she turned around when I walked in and smiled at me. She wiped her hands on her apron and swept across the room to feel up my baby bump.

"It's good to see you too," I said as she ran her hands over Elliot's bubble. He kicked and danced around, and I swear kitchen lady almost cried.

"I'm glad you are back." She hustled back to the cake and cut a big slice, slipping it onto a plate and setting it at the small table in the corner. "Come, sit."

Don't have to ask me twice. I parked my pants in front of the cake and munched on the delicious sweet treat. My eyes rolled back in my head as the soft cake hit my tongue. Kitchen lady hustled back over and set a cup of coffee down.

"Decaf," she said.

I crinkled my nose.

"It's good, you will like it," she promised. She returned to the stove to stir something in a large pot. I took a sip. She was right. Whatever kitchen lady had done to make the caffeine free coffee taste just as good as regular coffee, I wouldn't question it. I thought I would have to start drinking water or tea. When I finished my cake, I leaned back in my chair and let my body digest. I finally felt full, something that was getting harder to do as Elliot grew. Elliot was taking up so much space, it should be easier to get full, but it seemed like the opposite. He was growing so fast I needed to eat more.

"Happy birthday, Lark," the kitchen lady said as she took my plate away. I spent my birthday in a cave getting gored by a buffalo. Maybe I could pretend today was my birthday instead. I got to have a picnic and cake — sounds like a birthday.

"Thanks," I replied, and she went back to stirring.

It had been a long time since I had a birthday party. When I was young, my parents threw big birthday parties, but while I was in foster homes, it was never a huge deal. I could have a party though. I thought about it — streamers and balloons. A pinata. It wouldn't be a long game with the warriors here. Someone would chop it and then it would rain candy. I walked out of the kitchen, and as I passed the dining room, something caught my eye. I stopped and backed up a step, peeking through into the dining room. Someone hung balloons and streamers from the ceiling, and a giant pinata hung in the middle of the room. None of it was there when I walked by the first time. I looked around, but the vampires seemed as stunned as I was.

Oops.

I laughed. Whatever was going on with me now, I threw myself a birthday party — good thing I didn't wish for ponies. My laughter echoed through the halls and drew the attention of a few passing vampires.

Magic that grants wishes? Perfect. I continued down the hall and up the stairs to Vincent's room. Our room, I guess. I turned on the water in the tub, planning to have a hot bath. I walked back into the room to get clean clothes to change into, but there was a vampire in my room. An unhappy looking vampire. Vincent.

I raised an eyebrow at him.

"I don't think you should be running around town on a motorcycle. Particularly not with another man," he said.

I put one hand on my hip and stared him down. "Are you telling me what I can do and who I can be friends with?"

He scanned my face for a long moment, then looked away.

"That's what I thought," I said, moving to the closet to find clothes. When I came back, he was sitting on the bed, his head in his hands. Of course, I felt sorry for the poor bastard and sighed. I sat down on the bed beside him. "I'm with you, Vincent. We're going to get married and have a baby and live happily ever after."

He turned his head and looked at me.

"You know you can't boss me around. You're going to have to live with that," I said.

He nodded. "I'm sorry. I'm just worried. I know Frankie's a better man than I am."

"That's a load of shit. You are a good man — the best," I said, pushing him onto his back on the bed and climbing on so I was straddling his chest. "And you are mine." I kissed his nose, making him chuckle, then kissed his lips wiping the smile off his mouth. My tongue lashed out and swept across his sharp teeth before I pressed it onto the point of one, spilling a drop of blood in his mouth. He rolled over, pinning me under him and sucked on my tongue before pushing off me and standing up.

"What's wrong?" I asked.

"Nothing, I'm just hungry."

The way he said it, I knew he didn't mean he needed to order a pizza. "Then bite me."

He shook his head. "No way. You need all your blood for Elliot. I'm going to get a bag of blood from the supply." He turned toward the door.

"Are we ok?" I asked before he opened the door.

He turned back and smiled at me. "We'll always be ok. Even when we aren't ok."

I laughed, and he disappeared out the door. I sighed and lay back on the bed, remembering the way his hands slid over my hips. I remembered my bath and jumped up to check on the water. It was steaming hot, so I let some out and added cold water until it was an acceptable temperature and then lay back and relaxed among the mountains of bubbles. My stomach stuck up out of the water like a whale breaching the surface. I ran my hands over it, watching as Elliot rummaged around in there. I imagined him fighting monsters and saving the day like in comic books. Pow. Bam. My stomach had grown over the day, it could have been the burgers or cake, but it felt like all baby.

When the water cooled, I got out and dried off, wedging into some yoga pants and a hoodie, and went downstairs to find Vincent. He hadn't filled me in on his trip to the elves.

Downstairs I found Andre in the foyer signing for some packages and Trevor leaning over his shoulder trying to see the stack of boxes at the door.

"What's going on?" I asked.

Trevor spun around. "Nothing," he said way too fast.

I narrowed my eyes at him.

"Just let it be a surprise," he said.

I rolled my eyes. "OK, fine." I walked down the hall to Vincent's office and knocked once before swinging open the door.

Vincent sat behind his desk a pen in his hand, but his eyes on me. "Hey," I said, stepping in and closing the door behind me.

"Hi, you smell like flowers." He smiled, and the room lit up light a sunrise. His eyes danced and his pointy teeth twinkled.

I almost forgot why I came down here, but then I shook my head and told myself to stop drooling over my vampire. "What did you learn from the elves?"

He set down his pen and leaned back in his chair. "Nothing, Emanuel wouldn't talk to me."

"That's weird," I said, walking forward to sit in the chair in front of his desk.

"Not really, he's a strange fellow."

"Yeah. I remember," I said with a laugh. Then I filled Vincent in on what had been happening. The strange magical things that shouldn't happen.

"I think you should talk to Emanuel. It's important. The elves know things they don't share outside their kind."

"Do you think I'm an elf?" I asked.

"I don't think so, but who knows."

I nodded and stood to leave. I wasn't sure how to feel about being an elf or maybe part elf. Even though I had Durga inside me, I was still a human. I ran my hand over my stomach again. It was becoming strangely calming to have my hand on my belly.

"I hired a doctor for you. She is a vampire working a few cities over but agreed to come and be your doctor until after Elliot is born. She will be here tomorrow at noon."

"Thank you. I'll see Emanuel. I don't like not knowing what's going on."

"Take someone with you." Vincent rose and came around his desk. He handed me a cell phone. It was new and shiny. "I'll send directions to your phone. Try not to lose this one." His wry smile had my stomach doing flips that had nothing to do with the tiny ninja who lived in there. "I think Drew would probably appreciate the gesture if you wanted to take him along."

I nodded, and Vincent swooped down, sealing his lips to mine. I reached up and ran my fingers through his soft hair as our tongues twisted. When we finally broke away, we were both panting, and I didn't want to leave the office. The tiny couch in the corner looked plenty big enough for two.

He followed my line of sight and laughed. "I have to finish this paperwork. We can spend tonight in a much more comfortable bed."

"All right, but no take backs and no paperwork in bed." His laughter was the last sound I heard as the door swung shut behind me.

I took the hall to the TV room to see if I could find my buddy, Drew.

CHAPTER SIXTEEN

Drew jumped up. "Yes!"

"All right, you know we aren't killing anything right?"

"That's fine. I have always wanted to see an elf. This is going to be great! Just let me go grab my jacket." He ran off leaving me in the middle of the darkened entertainment room with a bunch of vampires staring at me. Now seemed like a good time to start getting to know the vampires.

"Nice to see you all," I said.

"Down in front," Peri called, throwing popcorn at me. I hadn't seen her back there.

"Oh my god, you suck," I said, as I scooted out of the way of the raining popcorn.

"That is a true statement. Meet me later for yoga," she grinned. I gave her a thumbs up, and they unpaused the movie. The vampires all went back to watching the car chase in progress on whatever action movie they were watching. It was nice to see that Peri was fitting in with the vampires of the house.

I found Andre in the foyer, talking on his phone. He flipped it shut when he saw me and a smile pulled onto his face.

"Hi Lark, I called down to the garage to have him send up your vehicle," he said.

"Great, thanks. How are you settling in?" I asked. It was nice to have another human here. If that was what I was.

"Good, everyone has been friendly," he replied, his eyes darting over my shoulder.

I turned around and found Trevor sitting on the bottom step of the stairs. "What are you doing here?" I asked.

"Just making sure Andre doesn't have any problems," he said, but his eyes stayed on Andre. Poor guy had a thing for the house human. At least it seemed mutual, judging by the look on Andre's face.

"Ready," Drew said as he sailed down the stairs pulling his jacket on. He leapt the last six steps and landed in the foyer beside me.

I was a bit jealous of his vamp skills. I felt as athletic as a potato since Durga left. I couldn't jump six steps and land without twisting an ankle or something. There was still bruising on my chest from the buffalo demon.

Andre opened the door and Drew, and I walked out to find a beige minivan in the driveway. I stopped dead and spun around.

"You are kidding me, right?" I asked the human in the doorway.

"Vincent just bought it yesterday. It's nice, right?" Andre said.

"I'm not driving that. Hold on Drew." I marched back into the house and slammed through Vincent's office door.

"Where is my SUV?" I asked, hands on my hips.

He muttered words into the phone at his ear, then set it down on the desk. "I traded it in. I thought you would want something safer for Elliot."

"The SUV was safe. A minivan is for soccer moms. Plus, you didn't even ask. That SUV drove me around all over the place. We had good times together."

"I didn't realize you had an emotional attachment to the vehicle."

"Yeah, well, that's because you didn't ask, Vincent. You traded it in without discussing anything with me."

He didn't speak for a moment. "I'm sorry." He stood up and came around his desk. He stepped right up to me, and I took a step back, not quite ready to accept his apology.

He took my hand and raised it to his lips. "I'm not used to this yet. Please be patient with me. I know I have to change, but I have been ruling over vampires for a long time. I've never had a partner."

"Is that what I am? A partner? Because I feel like I have no say in anything and I'm being towed along by life. I'm not deciding for myself."

All the air left Vincent's lungs. "Do you not want this? Our family?" His eyes dropped to my stomach.

"You idiot. I want a life with you, but I want to make my own decisions. Important things. You chose my doctor for me; you chose my car for me, I don't have a job or a bank account. I don't have anything."

"I've given you everything."

"Exactly. That's amazing and wonderful, but I want something that's mine. I think I need to rebuild my Yoga studio. I need some control over something."

"I put the insurance money from your old yoga studio in a trust account I set up for you. I didn't know if you would ever want it," he said.

Thoughts of Randy flooded into my mind. He built that studio more than I did. Could I use the insurance money to build a new studio? Should I? I couldn't decide if it would be honouring him or belittling his memory to rebuild like he hadn't lost his life in the last one. All the air left my lungs. I shook my head, trying to fight back the emotions attempting to boil over.

"I don't know how to do anything right," he whispered.

My eyes shot up to his. "No, that's good. I can use that, but I miss Randy sometimes. He was my biggest cheerleader. Maybe I could make it in his memory — make sure he lived on in a new studio."

Vincent wrapped his arms around me. "Ok. I'll put it in an account for you. Do you want me to contact architects? Or I could get you a list of names? I won't take over, but if I can help, I want to."

"A list of names would be good. If I'm not chasing down vampires, I will have time to call around."

"Ok. I can do that." His smile came back, tentative at first. I felt like a bitch for yelling at him now, but I wanted to work things out and be a team. We didn't have long before we would have a child. This was a jump first and learn to swim later thing. "Do you want to hire someone to help with the wedding? I think Trevor is planning something baby related."

I laughed remembering him and his secret boxes at the door — he was up to something.

"Yeah, how about you handle the wedding plans? Peri and I can go dress shopping after Elliot's born. I'm not getting married with a big belly."

He laughed, and we were back to normal. He kissed me and headed back to his desk. "You don't have any restrictions on the wedding?"

"What does that mean?" I asked, suspicious now.

"Well, we know many people." He said, flipping open his agenda and turning pages with a sharp slide of his fingers.

Oh god. There would be hundreds of people at this wedding. I just knew it. "Nope, I said you could do it, so whatever you want is fine."

He smiled and bit his lip. "I'll keep it small... ish." He said. I turned to leave, but before I pulled open the door, Vincent spoke again.

"I love you, Lark."

"I love you too," I said, shooting him a smile then heading back out to the parking lot to drive my freaking mini-van.

"Next right turn," the mechanical voice of my GPS said.

"Shit," I slipped into the right lane and screamed onto the off-ramp of the highway.

"I am going to die," Drew said, clinging to the door handle for dear life.

"No, you won't. This thing has like twenty airbags." I pulled up to the stop sign.

"Turn left," the mechanical voice said.

"I kind of love this GPS thing. My SUV didn't have this."

"So now you like the mini-van?" Drew asked rolling his eyes.

"No, but I like the features." It had heated seats. My ass had never been so toasty. It also had little TV's on the back of the front seats so kids could watch movies in the car. Pretty sweet deal.

We drove over the highway and through a cute little town. The houses were quaint with coloured doors and gardens.

"You have reached your destination," the tinny voice said, but I hadn't. There wasn't an address on the old logging road. I drove out of town watching the left-hand shoulder to find the overgrown path and cement barrier that prevented vehicles from driving up to where Emanuel's magic house.

"There it is." I spun the wheel and slammed to a stop inches from the barrier to the sound of Drew screaming like a little girl.

I put the van in park and hopped out. Drew followed a moment later.

"Can I drive home?" he asked. I snickered and fought my way through the branches that blocked the side of the path around the barrier. I wasn't about to hop over it. My stomach was full from the foot-long sandwich I had bought on the way here.

We walked through the wooded path, birds swooped and tweeted, hopping from branch to branch. The sun was shining, breaking through the trees now and then to heat my skin, and a warm breeze carried the scent of flowers along the path.

We walked for several minutes until we came to a small meadow. I knew the house was there.

"Emanuel?" I called, and before my eyes, the tiny cottage sprung into being — little flower boxes on the windows and a cute little-covered porch with a swinging bench. Perched on the bench was the little green leprechaun himself. Except he wasn't a leprechaun, and I knew better than to call him that.

"Hello, little Lark. Thank you for coming." The tiny man said. He took off his emerald green top hat and bowed at me.

"It's nice to see you again, Emanuel," I said.

"Come, you can bring this vampire if you must, but he should touch nothing," Emanuel said giving Drew a look like he was a little boy with sticky fingers.

I giggled and climbed the three small steps to Emanuel's cottage. He opened the door and disappeared inside. I followed along expecting to see the warehouse, but what was beyond the doors this time was completely different.

I walked into a huge room with vaulted ceilings and plush red carpet on an aisle between rows and rows of benches. It was like a church or opera house. On the benches, thousands of small people clapped and cheered. Lights poured in from some unseen source, illuminating the stage at the front of the magnificent room. On the stage, sat a chair I could only describe as a throne.

"Come, Lark. The people wait."

"What the hell?" I asked.

"Your son must receive his gift," Emanuel said, ushering me forward.

I stopped dead in my tracks. "I don't understand."

"You will." The elf smiled up at me and then took my hand before I could stop him. Suddenly, I was in a vision. I knew it wasn't real because I watched myself playing with Elliot. His beautiful face was lit up with smiles and giggles as he ran and I chased him. He put out his hand

and the tree in front of him changed. Its branches lowered until they formed steps he ran up and then the branches moved again, so he was standing in a tree fort, looking out the window at me. The sun sparkled on his face as it came through the leaves, casting him in a warm glow.

Then I was back in the giant room full of elves.

It was Elliot making the magic. Of course, he would be different. He is the son of a god. Relief flew through me. It wasn't me that was magic; it was him. Then the horrible thought struck me — he would grow up thinking he was strange just as I had when I was young and weird. At least he would have magic around him. Frankie had magic.

"He will be happy Lark. Come." Emanuel waved me forward, so I walked along the red carpet, Drew at my back until we climbed the stairs onto the stage. Emanuel encouraged me to sit in the giant chair, so I took a deep breath. I wasn't excited to be in front of so many people. I was wearing yoga pants and a hoodie that said baby with an arrow pointing down to my stomach. I found it in my closet this morning and thought was hilarious. I wasn't dressed to be in front of all these people and sitting on a damn throne.

"Thank you all for coming," Emanuel said, his voice echoing through the room and calming the cacophony of applause. "Today we welcome the mother of our new king. Though she is of humble birth, the great Goddess chose her, and now she bears the son of the King of Thunder. This child will be more powerful than any before. Help me give him the gift he needs to grow into the powerful leader of our people."

Emanuel turned to me. "Thank you, young Lark. We will meet again." He raised his arms. I was about to ask him what he meant when a wave of gold light began at the back of the room and slid above the rows of people. I grew in size and speed as it made its way towards the stage. The people all had their arms raised, and they cheered as the wave crashed over them and continued. I tried to stand, but some force held me in place. The golden wave crashed onto the stage, and I opened my mouth to scream, but it was too late. It hit me and washed over me and the chair I was sitting on, but it had no weight. It was like fog, I could see it, but I couldn't feel it. A moment later it all disappeared, and I was sitting in the same throne in the middle of the empty forest clearing. The room and the people had vanished, except Drew who stood beside me with a look of utter disbelief. It probably matched my own. What the fuck?

"That was weird." Trust Drew to state the obvious.

I stood up from the chair, and something fell out of my lap. When I bent down, the chair behind me disappeared. I picked up the shiny object and held it up. It was a tiny crown, not much bigger than a bracelet.

It was a crown for a baby.

CHAPTER SEVENTEEN

The ride home was quiet. I let Drew take the driver's seat, and he drove like a grandma. My stomach was pretty freaking huge now. So big that I set the tiny crown on it like it was a shelf and watched the writhing mass that warped my skin with cramped ninja moves.

My hoodie stretched tight across my stomach. I wasn't sure I would be able to get it off when I got home. I made Drew stop and get me a snack. I munched on Cheesies, crunching loudly and chugged a sports drink as I kept vigil on the tiny crown and my giant stomach.

Once we were back on the highway, I pulled out my cell phone and took a picture of the crown on my belly. I almost posted it to my neglected social media page, but couldn't remember my password, so I texted it to Vincent and Peri.

Peri replied first. Telling me that my belly was huge, and I needed to lay off the snacks. She's a good friend.

Vincent called.

"Is that what they gave you?" he asked without so much as a hello.

"Yup, Emanuel said Elliot was their new king, and then they threw a bunch of gold stuff at me and kicked me out of their house. The crown was on my lap."

"They threw a bunch of gold stuff at you?" He asked, sounding confused. I was just as confused.

"Yeah, like magic or something. Now my stomach is quite a bit bigger, so we might need that baby room before soon."

"I scheduled the contractor to start the door between rooms tomorrow. If the room isn't ready, he can stay in our room. I would like that anyway."

"You would?" I asked. I never thought of Vincent being a hands-on father.

"Absolutely. The two of you sleeping in my room sounds perfect."

"OK, well, we should be home soon," I said with a giddy smile on my face.

"See you soon," he said.

We hung up, and I went back to my snack. I had orange powder all over my stomach by the time we pulled into the mansion. I tried to dust it off, but it was permanent. I rolled out of the van and up the stairs to the front door. It swung open to reveal Andre. He bowed his head. "Lord Vincent would like to see you in the dining room."

"Lord Vincent," I said in a mocking tone, "Will have to wait because I have to pee," I said — too much sports drink. I should have had coffee. I wouldn't have this problem. Coffee never betrayed me by filling my bladder unnecessarily.

I hustled past Andre to the small half bath tucked away behind the staircase, making it just in time. Damn, being pregnant sucked.

I waddled back out of the bathroom, cursing my expanded waistline and found the foyer empty. So, I staggered down the hall towards the dining room, carrying the tiny crown in my hand. I didn't want to set it down somewhere and lose it. I turned the corner into the dining room, and everyone yelled "surprise" so loud I was glad I had just emptied my bladder.

They decorated the room better than my birthday streamers. There were soft blue streamers, but also a giant sign that said congratulations in blue letters and balloons everywhere. Elliot did an epic flip, and I got a stabbing pain in my back. Little turnip needed to settle down. Everyone was clapping, and Trevor was taking pictures.

I shook my head at the goofy vampire, but he ushered me forward to a chair decorated with balloons and puffy plastic pompoms. When I sat down, everyone came over and set gifts down around me. This was way over the top.

Vincent came up and stood beside me. "This is from me," he said, handing me a tiny box.

I looked up at him in his handsome suit and tie and his hair perfectly styled. Then I looked down at my huge belly covered in orange cheese powder. God, I was a hippopotamus.

I took his tiny box and pulled the wrapping off. The box said Tiffany. I took the top off and inside was a gold necklace with a beautiful lightning bolt encrusted with diamonds. It was fitting since I gave him Indra's lightning bolt that Durga carried around with her.

"Thank you," I whispered. He took it and stood behind my chair. I swept my hair out of the way, and he attached it around my neck. It was beautiful the way it sparkled.

"Ok, now open mine," Trevor said, shoving a gift in my lap. I had another sharp stabbing pain in my back and winced then took Trevor's beautifully wrapped present. It was rather large, and the blue paper had hearts on it that said: "It's a boy."

I tore at the paper. Some heckler yelled at me to hurry up, and I looked up to find Peri standing on a table, smiling at me from the other side of the dining room.

I shook my head at her and tore the paper. Inside was something called a diaper genie.

"You put diapers in it," Trevor said excitedly.

"It's a magic poo garbage?" I asked.

He nodded and put another present in my lap, setting the diaper genie aside.

I opened several more gifts. Little cute outfits and toys and all kinds of things I had no idea a baby needed, but the pain in my back was getting worse.

"Ok, guys, I love this, and you guys are all too sweet, but my back is killing me, and I would like to go lay down," I said. "Can we pick this up again later?"

Everyone clapped and cheered as Vincent helped me up from my chair. Trevor had been making me a ridiculous hat from bows and ribbons on a paper plate. I had no interest in wearing it. Shockingly.

As I stood up, I felt a huge gush.

"Shit," I said.

"Oh my god, your water broke," Trevor yelled.

I knew enough about birth to know this baby was coming today and that is the moment reality set in.

"I'm having a baby," I said. The vampires all cheered again. Bunch of idiots. The pain in my back morphed into agony, and I was ready to throat punch everyone who didn't get out of my way.

"Move," Vincent yelled, clearing me a path as I waddled out of the dining room. He had his phone to his ear the moment he passed me off to Trevor and Peri, who slung their arms around me and helped me out of the room. They moved me towards the medical room, and I slammed on the breaks.

"No way, I'm having this baby in my bed, not in that room."

I had seen so many injured vampires in there. Trevor was there when he came home with me and after the rogues attacked him. I didn't want to have my baby in that cold, stark room.

"Ok, Lark, up the stairs we go. Just take them one step at a time." I lifted my foot to set it on the first stair but Vincent swept me off my feet and carried me in his strong arms.

"Frankie is picking up your doctor. She will be here in a few minutes."

I nodded, but the pain was much worse, and I could hardly breathe.

"Lark, breath like me," Trevor said making a puff sound. I copied him. It sounded ridiculous. Vincent set me down on the bed and tried to kick everyone out.

"Leave them alone," I moaned. I didn't want Elliot to be born with his dad yelling at people.

Suddenly, Frankie and a woman in surgical scrubs appeared in my room.

"Hey Lark. This is Doctor Foster," Frankie said.

The doctor was a vampire. She smiled at me and came to the side of the bed. Vincent watched on from the end of the bed, his body tense like he thought he might have to fight someone.

"Hi, nice to meet you," I said before another sharp pain shot through me making me groan. The doctor was speaking, but I couldn't focus on anything but the pain. Where was Durga now? I could use a little of her magic. This hurt like hell.

"All right, anyone who is staying can stand by Lark's head. Anyone who is leaving, please leave now, this baby is on its way." Dr. Foster took control of the room, and everyone did as she asked, even Vincent. It wasn't long before she told me to push and I pushed for all I was worth.

It seemed like hours. My matted hair stuck to my face with sweat, and every part of me hurt, but Dr. Foster said one last push and Elliot was born. I lay back on the bed and stared up at Vincent, but he looked worried. His eyes were on the end of the bed. I struggled onto my elbows. Realizing everyone was staring at the little bundle the doctor was rubbing.

"What's wrong?" I asked.

The blanket moved, and I realized the baby I had given birth to was blue.

"Why does he look like that? Shouldn't he be screaming or something?" I looked back, and Trevor had his hand over his mouth.

"What's wrong?" I asked more forcefully. "What is wrong with Elliot?"

The doctor didn't look up; she kept pressing on Elliot's little chest. The blanket moved again, and I saw his little face, eyes closed like an angel.

That wasn't right. I had seen him as a boy.

I panicked. My heart screamed in my chest. He had to be ok. I tried to find Durga or reach Shiva, but they weren't here. It was just me, and I had no magic. I remembered the words Emanuel said. The gift he needs to grow into a powerful leader of our people.

"The crown," I said. "Where is the crown?"

Everyone looked at me like I was crazy, but Vincent pulled it out of his pocket and left my side. He stopped the doctor's efforts and when she leaned back; he leaned forward and placed the tiny crown on Elliot's peach fuzz covered head.

The crown disappeared in a ring of golden smoke, and suddenly Elliot took a deep, ragged breath and screamed. His body turned from blue to pink a moment later, and his arms flailed. My body took over, and I scooped him off the bed to hold him on my chest. His screams quieted and his sky-blue eyes locked on mine for the first time. My heart melted into a red goo in my chest. I cradled the most perfect being in my arms. I pulled my blanket up to tuck him in tight to my chest and kissed his beautiful forehead. He was all gooey and gross and perfect. I counted his little fingers and lay back on the pillows. He stared into my eyes while I studied him.

People moved around the room, but I couldn't have broken my eyes away from the tiny being in my arms if I wanted too.

"Lark," Vincent's voice whispered beside me. Elliot's eyes shifted from me to Vincent, breaking the trance. Vincent was smiling at me. "Dr. Foster would like to check him and you out. I thought perhaps Trevor could bath him while the doctor makes sure you are all right?"

My eyes shot to Trevor. I reminded myself that I trusted Trevor; he would never hurt our baby, but I still had this irrational urge to keep Elliot in my arms.

"I will guard him with my life, Lark," the Russian accented voice of Ninel rang through the room, and I took a deep breath. Still wary, I handed Elliot to Vincent who held him while Dr. Foster listened to his heart and felt his stomach. I couldn't see Elliot's face from my angle, but I saw his tiny hand wrap around Vincent's finger. A tear tipped over Vincent's eyelid to run down his cheek, but his smile nearly split his face in two.

When the doctor finished, Vincent handed Elliot to Trevor, who set him down and wrapped him up in a blanket, so he was a tiny sausage. Ninel stood at Trevor's side. The contrast between the tiny baby and the massive vampire warrior was astonishing. Even though Ninel was still thin, he towered over everyone in the room, and he had a sword strapped to his broad shoulders. I had seen him swing the sword battle and decapitate many fallen vampires. I knew he would keep my baby safe.

Once the doctor checked me out and gave me the all clear, she handed me a couple painkillers and went to get settled into her room. Vincent asked her to stay for a month so that I would have a doctor on hand.

"So, this was really gross," Peri said, flopping down on the bed beside me but strategically staying out of the bloody mess that giving birth had made.

"It was magical, and you know it," I said, smiling at her.

"Ok, it was kinda magical," she agreed. "But let's not do this again."

"Agreed."

"Congratulations, you two," Frankie said. I had forgotten he was here, he was in the far corner of the room, looking awkward.

"Thanks, Frankie," I said.

Trevor and Ninel came back a few minutes later with my sausage baby and handed him to Vincent. I could smell the baby shampoo they had used on him. He smelled like baby powder.

"Ok, everyone out, I want time with my family," Vincent said in a soft voice that somehow lacked none of his usual authority even though it was quiet.

Frankie took hold of Peri's hand, and the two of them disappeared, everyone else walked out the door. Vincent helped me off the bed to sit me on a chair and set Elliot in my arms. Then he stripped the bed and replaced the sheets and blankets while I stared down at our perfect baby sleeping in my arms.

Then he helped me into the clean, fresh bed. Vincent lay beside me, and I set our perfect boy between us. We both stared at him for what seemed like hours or maybe just a moment. Vincent played with Elliot's tiny fingers, and I ran my hand over his soft downy hair.

"He's so perfect," I whispered.

"You are perfect," Vincent said, and I looked up to realize he was staring at me.

"No way. I am nothing compared to Elliot. He is perfect."

Vincent leaned in and kissed me, careful not crush our sleeping baby. Then he leaned down and kissed Elliot's brow, and we lay there in peaceful quiet until I fell asleep.

CHAPTER EIGHTEEN

"Congratulations, young Lark. Your child is quite precious." I was somehow in Shiva's temple, Elliot swaddled in my arms.

Shiva's snake slid forward and stuck out its tongue. I held Elliot closer to my chest and narrowed my eyes at the snake.

"Come now, my serpent won't harm your child," Shiva said with a laugh.

"How did I get here, I thought I couldn't come now that Durga has left me," I said. Elliot's perfect little features pulled my eyes back to him. He stared with more awareness then I thought was normal for a newborn.

"Durga hasn't left you," Shiva said. "She is just resting and didn't want to disturb the growth of your beautiful boy. Now that he has come into the world, I'm sure she will make her way back to you. When the time is right."

A chill ran down my spine. Maybe I wouldn't have the quiet life of a yoga instructor after all. "When is that likely to be?" I asked.

"Someday. I dare not speak for the goddess. She does not like it when I do."

I smiled. It was kind of funny that the great God Shiva feared Durga's anger. Though, I supposed she was kind of scary.

"Come to me when you have problems, I will be available to you. Now goodbye young Lark. Take care of your precious boy. I have important work to do."

✳ ✳ ✳

I opened my eyes to find Vincent sitting on the bed beside me. He was leaning back against the headboard, his legs stretched out and Elliot in his arms.

He smiled at me, and Elliot made a tiny coo. I sat up and scooted back, so I was leaning against the headboard beside him. Then gazed down at our cute little munchkin. I could stare at him all day. I wondered if all new mothers felt this way. It was actual love at first sight. I had never experienced it before, and it was overwhelming.

"I have to go away for a few days," Vincent said.

"What? Now?" I asked.

"Yes. Our little guy here has upset the Elders of the magic community. They have a long-standing feud with the elves and aren't happy that I'm now the father of their king. The magic people think I have joined forces with the elves, and we are planning a takeover. It's ridiculous. I need to smooth things over with the elders, and then I will be back here with you two."

"Why do you have to go? Can't you send Peri? That's her job, right? Magical liaison."

Vincent studied me for a minute and then sighed. "You're right." He kissed the top of my head. "I hired her for a job. I should let her do it. She has a sense of tact sometimes, and she is old enough they will respect her word. I have a control problem."

I laughed. "That is an understatement."

"Do you see what I have to put up with?" he said to Elliot, laughing.

"You will find no sympathy from him. I'm the mom, and I am always right." I reached over and scooped Elliot out of Vincent's arms. "Isn't that right Eli?"

"I like Eli. I was trying to come up with a shorter version of his name. Elliot is as much of a mouthful as Vincent."

I studied his profile for a second. "Why don't you shorten your name? Vinny?" I laughed. Oh no, he was not a Vinny.

"That's why. Vinny doesn't suit me, but it suits Elliot to be Eli."

We both watched as Eli swung his hand around like he was casting a spell. God, he was cute.

"All right, I better go find Peri and let her know she will talk to the elders," Vincent said, pushing off the bed. "I'll send up food for you. Rest for today at least? Trevor said he would be glad to change diapers and feed Eli."

"Ok, thank you."

I watched Vincent stride across the room and out the door before my eyes slipped back to my little bundle. "So, you are all magic and stuff, huh?" Eli cooed again, his little mouth in a tiny circle. "Is that so? Well, just remember that mommy doesn't have magic, so please don't make me chase you around too much. Ok?"

Eli smiled. I don't care what anyone says it was a wicked grin if ever there was one.

I was in so much trouble. I laughed anyway.

This might be the best adventure yet.

* * *

Peri

The gym in the house was excellent, and the supply of good fighters was nearly endless. Vincent had a good, disciplined workforce.

I jumped into a roundhouse kick, knocking the vampire I was sparring with on his ass. He leaped back to his feet before he ever really settled on his back. Quick. I liked that. I threw an arm out towards his head, but he ducked in time and landed a quick jab to my solar plexus, radiating pain through my core muscles. I swept out my leg, catching his front weight bearing leg, and he collapsed like an old house in an earthquake. A smile pulled my lips as I threw myself down, fist first to his face.

"Stop." The commanding voice of my new city lord rang through the gym.

Too late to keep my sparring partner from bleeding everywhere, but I pulled the second punch, so the chap only had a bloody lip and a broken nose, not a fractured jaw to go with it.

I stood up and turned towards Vincent. "We were just having some fun," I said.

The guy on the floor groaned and rolled onto his side. Ok, so I was having fun.

"I see that you have found a way to keep yourself busy."

"You don't have any rogues or fallen in the city, just keeping my skills sharp," I said with a grin. One of my teeth had been knocked out in an earlier sparring match. Not a canine, I would have been angry if he had knocked out one of my good chompers, but it was just an incisor. It would grow back but made me look badass, having the gap, I was sure.

Vincent shook his head. "Can I talk to you in my office?" he asked, turning to go before I answered him.

I looked down at the bloody vampire at my feet. "I better not be in trouble because you are playing dead."

The other vampire sprung to his feet and laughed as he walked away. Asshole.

I grabbed a towel and wiped the sweat off my brow as I walked out of the gym and down the hall to Lord Vincent's office.

His office was kind of like him, uptight and straight edge. I wasn't sure what Lark saw in him until I saw the man shed a tear at the birth of his son. Then I caught a tiny glimpse of how different he was with Lark. I wondered if that was all an act or if this tough-stick-in-the-mud Vincent was the act. Either way, I wasn't sure I liked him that much, so my confusion stands.

"You wanted to see me?" I said, standing in front of his desk.

"Yes, I assigned you as liaison to the magical community, but I didn't realize that this role would ever become so vital. As you might be aware, the magic community and the elves have a long-standing distrust for each other due to some feud that began long ago."

I nodded, I had heard about it, though I wasn't around when the wars waged. That was before Vincent's time too.

"The magic community has raised an issue with me fathering the king of the elves. They think this is a sign that the vampires are switching allegiance, and I can't have a war on my doorstep. I worked hard to forge an alliance with the witches and warlocks. This is also terrible timing. Lark needs me around right now, so I would like you to go with Frankie, as our liaison, and meet with the elders. Assure them we are not changing anything and still wish to remain neutral in their war."

"Sure, sounds like fun."

Vincent bit his lip and rubbed his forehead. "I'm not happy about sending anyone, but I don't know you Peri, and I am less happy about sending you. I would send my brother, Vlad, but he has gone home to visit my twin, and this won't wait." He paused and held my eye contact. It was very dramatic. "Please don't start a war with the magical community."

"No worries, boss. I got this." He was still rubbing his forehead like he had a headache. "Is that all?" I asked.

"Yes, you are dismissed."

He didn't look up, so I toddled on my way. I took a shower and changed into some ass kicking clothes, strapped my knife on my leg and then tucked a few more in strategic locations on my body. I sent a text to Frankie that read. "You and me on a field trip to see the old witches?"

He replied "Really? I expected Vincent to handle this himself."

"Well, he has a tiny person to take care of, so I'm up," I sent.

"Awesome. You ready to go now?" he asked.

"Yes. Road trip!"

This would be a blast.

Jen Pretty
Visit my website at www.jenprettyauthor.com

Printed in the United States of America

First Printing: Jan 2019

ISBN-9781775290674